Perfect Shot

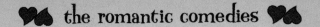
the romantic comedies

Perfect Shot

DEBBIE RIGAUD

Simon Pulse

New York London Toronto Sydney

SIMON PULSE

An imprint of Simon & Schuster Children's Publishing Division
1230 Avenue of the Americas, New York, NY 10020
First Simon Pulse paperback edition December 2009
Copyright © 2009 by Debbie Rigaud
All rights reserved, including the right of reproduction in
whole or in part in any form.
SIMON PULSE and colophon are registered trademarks of
Simon & Schuster, Inc.
For information about special discounts for bulk purchases,
please contact Simon & Schuster Special Sales
at 1-866-506-1949 or business@simonandschuster.com.
The Simon & Schuster Speakers Bureau can bring authors
to your live event. For more information or to book
an event contact the Simon & Schuster Speakers Bureau
at 1-866-248-3049 or visit our website
at www.simonspeakers.com.
Designed by Ann Zeak
The text of this book was set in Garamond 3.
Manufactured in the United States of America
10 9 8 7 6 5 4 3 2 1
Library of Congress Control Number 2009927872
ISBN 978-1-4169-7835-0
ISBN 978-1-4169-8551-8 (eBook)

To my mother, "Mummy,"
who loved to read;
my godmother, "Dada,"
who loved to write;
and my grandmother, "Mummum,"
who loved to tell stories

Acknowledgments

A soul-deep thank-you to my husband, Bernard, for inspiring me in so many ways. And to my family—Pappy, Shirley, Judy, Golda, Jerry, Natasha, Vanessa, Jessica, Fifie, and Micheline—for their awesome support and encouragement. Thanks to my father-in-law, Kwaku, for sharing stories from his high school teaching experience. A shout to my own teen advisory board: Ana, Victoria, Amanda, and Jamal Jr. A special thanks to the middle grade/high school teachers, librarians, and bookstore owners of Bermuda for welcoming me and introducing me to new readers. Utmost gratitude to Michael del Rosario, a gifted editor who understands my characters, and to my fabulous agent, Adrienne Ingrum, for believing in me.

One

"Heads up!" was my only warning before it was launched over the aisle toward me. Even though I was on one knee, stocking shelves with acrylic paint tubes, my reflexes were on their feet. My long forearms met the ball of rubber bands with a force that sent it hurling back toward where it came from.

"Ouch!" Pam, my coworker-slash-best-friend, yelped.

Snickering to myself, I rushed over to her aisle to apologize. She gave me the dramatic, injured look, so I knew it wouldn't be easy.

"C'mon, it was just a few *soft* rubber bands," I offered sweetly.

"Yeah—and *not* a volleyball." She pouted,

rubbing her forehead. "I swear, London, from now on, going to one of your volleyball matches is gonna feel like watching a scary movie."

"Seeing as how you overact worse than a Hollyweird D-lister," I teased, "that would be a step up for you."

Pam forgot about her wounded act and coughed up a boisterous laugh that I'm sure all of northern New Jersey heard. She's not usually the loud type, but the girl *is* known to turn up the volume on just about every aspect of her personality.

"You're never gonna let me live that down, huh?" Pam placed her hand—the one not holding a stack of colored pencils—over her heart and squinted as if the sun was in her eyes. "I did it for you. The ref had to understand how foul his call was."

Her theatrics aside, I appreciate that she comes to almost every one of my home games to show her support.

"Mmm-hmm," I teased. "Next time you get the urge to run screaming across the court during game time, don't do me any favors."

"Owww," Pam whimpered. Going for the right distraction to change the subject, she started stroking her forehead again. I grinned and wrapped my long arms around Pam's shoulders, giving her a quick, apologetic squeeze. My five-foot-ten frame extended half a head taller than her.

"Sorry." I picked up the rubber orb and carefully pulled off the red band on top. "Anyway, I only asked you for *one*."

"Next time I won't be so generous." Pam got in the last word before she carried on placing colored pencils into separate slots on a fixture.

I smiled to myself and headed back to my acrylic paint duties. Without intending it to be, working the same shift at Art Attack was becoming the perfect chance for Pam and me to hang together. Even though we're both sophomores at Teawood High, my volleyball season being in full swing and Pam's double passions for fashion *and* her boyfriend Jake have kept us preoccupied. Before this job, we'd mostly been keeping in touch via text.

Unexpected bonus BFF time aside, Pam got me a job here for another reason altogether. Once she heard I was passed up for the volleyball summer camp scholarship and had to raise the fifteen-hundred-dollar fee on my own, she put in a good word with her boss. Now here I am, two weeks later, proudly rocking the faux-paint-splattered, red employee vest.

Art Attack was one of a few artsy stores to pop up on Main Avenue in recent months. The seven-block strip, known to locals as "the Ave," always had potential. Just a few miles from New York City, Teawood, New Jersey, is a large suburb with a metropolitan vibe. Cozy coaches—or as we like to call them, adult school buses—make their way down the Ave, shuttling Teawood residents to and from their New York City jobs every workday morning and evening. On Saturdays kids either head across the bridge to shop in Manhattan or parade down the Ave in celebs-on-a-coffee-run attire. For them it's all about comfy boots with over-size handbags and shades.

In the heart of the strip, the brick sidewalks are spacious and lined with benches and old-world lampposts. Luxury car dealerships, designer shoe stores, and fancy evening gown showrooms stand alongside busy restaurants, open-late ice cream shops, and trendy clothing stores. Lots of famous folks who live in nearby, more upscale towns—

including a few rappers who publicly claim to still be living in New York City—can be spotted shopping or lunching here. (Reverend Run's kids are known to pass through, reality show cameras in tow.) Shiny cars cruise up and down, looking for both attention and parking.

No celebrity sightings in Art Attack to report yet. That's probably because my part-time working hours are spent avoiding customers and their art-related questions. Pam, in her artsyliciousness, is a much better fit for this job. Honestly, if I'd known that a prerequisite for working at an art supply store was creativity, I would've found another way to earn the money.

But it's all worth it. The Peak Performance Volleyball Camp in upstate New York trains top high school players from the tristate area and gives them a shot at making the national team. I've wanted to go to Peak Performance camp ever since my gym teacher told me about it in the eighth grade. It has the best reputation. Plus it lands athletes on the radar of prominent college scouts—which is right where I want to be.

Trust, I would walk around stuffed to the gills in grills like rapper Plies if you told me gold teeth had transmitters that blip on the radar of college scouts.

Crazy ambition aside, what's fun about Peak Performance is that after weeks of intensive training in the art of spiking, blocking, serving, and winning, the camp squad flies to Miami to play against teams from other regions across the country.

Even though scholarships were awarded to only two star athletes from my school—seniors who have already been handpicked to play volleyball in college—I was selected to join the camp. My parents said they'd gladly pay the hefty fee . . . but only if I enroll the summer *after* my junior year. Trouble is, who even knows what chance I'd have for getting picked next year! Considering there's no guaranteed placement, I just can't pass up this summer's opportunity.

So for now I'm all about improving my game, which it turns out, has been the therapy I needed to get over my ex-boyfriend Rick Stapleton. *Correction*: I didn't need to get over *him*, so much as the humiliation of being dumped publicly. Of course, all of that intensified volleyball focus has been reflected by my wardrobe (I pair a v-ball jersey with jeans, like, every day) and the number of v-ball clips on my Facebook page.

I'm finally shaking off the heartbreak, but I still feel stupid when I think of how, right before it went down, I was beaming like SpongeBob because I was genuinely happy for my then boyfriend. Picture gullible me, all chipper in the bleachers, watching Rick get honored as Peak Performance's Top Athlete in his age group. I jumped up and cheered so loudly when his name was announced that I gave myself laryngitis *and* a migraine. That was mere minutes before I found out that Rick had also worked on his playa-playa game during his summer away.

Yup, in August Rick returned from camp with a new girlfriend—the hot v-ball star from a rival school. After practically skipping off the bleachers, intending to congratulate Rick and welcome him back with a kiss, I caught the sight of him hugging up on a Keke Palmer look-alike. He didn't even unglue himself from her when he saw me staring, frozen in shock. It didn't matter, because by then my voice was too hoarse (and my head too achy) to confront Rick.

We haven't spoken since.

But despite the prime-time shaft—witnessed by the entire athletic student body, by the way—I'm turning things around. It's October, and I've established myself as a new, strong player on Teawood High School's varsity squad. Not even the sight of Unslick Rick watching from the stands (with *her*) can throw off my game.

"London Abrams, you're on register." My manager's squawky voice yanked me back from my daydream.

I noticed that I'd been squeezing a helpless tube of paint, leaving it misshapen and crinkled. As best I could, I flattened it to its near-original figure before placing it at the back of the shelf behind the undamaged tubes.

My boss didn't notice—he's in his own world. While other managers and employees of Art Attack are funky, creative types, this one is offbeat in a chop-off-an-ear van Gogh way. The poor guy seems tormented by a million unfinished personal art projects. He wears that torment in his hair. It looks more mad scientist than everyone else's bed-head vogue.

"*Great*, my favorite place to be," I said sarcastically, sidestepping his attempt at authority. With a million different possible payment transactions—cash, credit card,

Art Attack bonuses, promotional codes, coupons, employee discounts, buy-two-get-one-half-off deals—I still wasn't completely comfortable manning the checkout counter.

"Would you rather advise customers on how to put their art projects together?" he asked.

I suck at art advice. So, after stocking the shelves, I went to relieve the lanky goth guy signing off of register 1.

Fortunately for me, it was smooth sailing for the first two hours—just simple cash and credit card customers. But about a half hour before my lunch break, things started getting busy. The checkout lane signs—wide lamp shades displaying red numbers—blocked the shorter cashiers from view. On the flip side, my head towered above my lane's sign. Because they could see me, customers assumed I was the only employee on duty. So a long line formed at my register, while my coworkers at registers 2 and 3 seemed to be hiding behind their signs on purpose.

Just when I thought my boss would take notice of what was going on, an inquisitive customer whisked him away on a calligraphy ink hunt. It was up to me to handle the situation. I still had too much of that new-employee uneasiness to call out my coworkers, so I addressed the customers instead.

"Registers two and three are also open," I informed the back of the coiling line.

My announcement totally backfired. A cutie had been heading to my line, but just as I said this, he queued up behind the two customers who had also just switched to register 2. *Dang*. Curious, I stole a quick glance at him. He struck me as a cross between a teenage Lenny Kravitz and a modern-day Jean-Michel Basquiat. (Yes, working here has taught me a thing or two about famous dead hipster artists.) Dressed in a plaid button-down and khakis, he looked retro and current at the same time.

In the two weeks that I'd been an Art Attack employee, I'd come to recognize the look of a person with creative swagger. And Kravitz Cakes's air of creativity was more timeless than most hot-for-the-moment, trendy customers who pass through. Something about him made me want to act supergirlie, like twirl my hair around my finger or tilt back my head while laughing. I think it's called "flirting."

I wanted to meet this guy. For one, he

was taller than me—and possibly a full two inches taller at that. A lot of guys my age seem ten times more likely to catch mono than a growth spurt, so it's nice to come across a tall boy. Second—and this was huge—the mere fact that a guy caught my attention meant I must have been getting over Unslick Rick.

I started ringing up customers at double speed. I couldn't move faster if my name was Taylor Swift. Forget the checkout counter small talk I'd normally have. I just wanted the cutie to switch back to my lane when he realized it was the quicker option.

Funny how total strangers operate on the same timetable without even realizing it. There were solid blocks of time when not a soul walked into Art Attack. Then suddenly, as if a sightseeing tour bus had pulled up and parked outside the door, folks swarmed in all around the same time.

My coworker at register 2 and I both had two customers waiting in line. The cutie was at the end of her line. As she rang up stuff, I stole a glance over my shoulder to her lane like a paranoid marathon runner. She had two more items to ring up—a roll of satin ribbons and a box of fancy transparent paper, apparently for a bride to be into DIY wedding invitations.

Yes, I thought. *Those items take mad long to ring up because the UPC has to be typed in.*

The two high-pitched beeps I heard in the next heartbeat meant that my coworker had somehow successfully managed to scan the wrinkled sticker codes on both packages. In a panic, I scanned my remaining three items and totaled the purchase. In a rare retail move (and without once removing his dark shades), my customer handed me glorious exact change.

The cutie looked over with anticipation when he noticed my now shorter lane. He took a step in my direction when, out of nowhere, a trio of loud Jersey types beat him to the punch. Only one of them was purchasing anything, but the obnoxious group made my lane look extra crowded.

"I *know*," one of the women heaved out in a raspy smoker's voice. "I would just *die-yah* if they had it—I'm *tawkin'* flat out *die-yah*."

Then, like a killer block at the net to save the game, my boss walked up and pulled through.

"We have that size of canvas panels you

asked for in stock," he told the trio. "It'll be out in a few minutes if you want to wait for it."

The raspy-voiced woman was so excited, she did almost *die-yah*. Her painful attempt to squeal with delight threw her into a coughing fit. Once she recovered, the excited group christened the store manager a *"dawll"* as he led them down a side aisle.

This time His Royal Hotness acted fast and moved to my lane just as I handed my outgoing customer his receipt. *Yes!* If daydreams could come true, I would jump over the Sharpie-marked counter into his waiting arms.

For all my effort to come face-to-face with him, I didn't think of anything clever to say to Mr. Crushtastic. I barely managed to greet him. He had such a quiet intensity that it felt like anything I said would've sounded silly. For one, he was as focused as I get when I'm on the court. Dude carefully examined each photo matting tool as he placed them on the counter. I recognized that need to concentrate on the details to get the job done right. I'm the same way when it comes to volleyball. And from what I could tell, this guy was heavy into his photography game.

The safest thing for me to do was ring him up in silence. Suddenly, I felt self-conscious and wished I hadn't worn my faded powder-blue jersey. It made my deep brown skin look totally washed-out. Plus my Teyana Taylor thick, curly hair was wrestled into a messy ponytail as proof that I hadn't consulted the mirror enough while I styled it.

Fly Guy expected me to announce the grand total, but when I said nothing, he squinted at the glowing digital numbers on the register's screen. *Real smooth, London.* I wanted to throw the lamp-shade lane sign over my head and pretend I was a fixture. But for some reason, he was the one who looked embarrassed enough for the both of us. *Could I be making him nervous?* I wondered.

"Oh no," he said to himself, barely loud enough for me to hear. His stone-serious face softened into a grimace. "I'm short two bucks," he told me apologetically as he dug into his jeans pockets twice. "Uh . . . I could come back and pay you in two minutes, or I can just put something back and pick it up later . . . ," he rambled.

"No, it's okay," I heard myself say. "It's

no biggie. I'll just use a promotional code and that should cover it." I made up what I was saying as I went along. Meanwhile, my internal conversation went something like: *Why did I just decline his offers to swing by later? I just closed off my chance to see him again!*

"Thank you." He paused, looking at me as if for the first time. My stomach flip-flopped. The paper shopping bag I'd packed crinkled as he bashfully picked it up. Apparently our sudden stillness (and the sound of the bag) signaled to the waiting customer that it was time to ring up his manga artist brush-pen set and drawing pad. He slapped them onto the counter.

Nudged out, my crush turned away and walked out of the store.

Like a game-ending buzzer to a losing team, the door chime announcing his exit put me in a slight funk.

Two

"Earth to London." Pam waved her hands in front of my face. "*Gurl*, if you don't hurry up . . ."

I guess I had zoned out after the unidentified-fly-object-of-my-affection sighting.

When I finally snapped out of it, I moved from behind the counter to follow Pam. Her timing couldn't have been more perfect—I needed to step out for a break.

Pam and I were almost at the door when I backtracked. I'd forgotten to take off my Art Attack vest. "Wait here," I said to an impatient Pam.

A few seconds later, right after I'd hung my vest on the hook and was nearing Pam, it hit me that I'd forgotten something else. I did an about-face again.

"Oh, no, no, no," Pam whined. "Whatever you forgot, do it when you get back. Our hour's practically over as it is."

I looked at the time on my cell and saw that we'd only used up four minutes of the lunch break. "You're so dramatic," I told her before jogging back to my post.

My intention was to open my register and place the two wrinkled dollar bills from my wallet on top of the pile of ones. But Goth Guy beat me there by a few paces. Where he came from, I had no idea.

Definitely not a good time to make that move, I thought.

Goth Guy looked like he expected me to ask him a new-girl question. I played it off by peering down an aisle as if searching for someone. After a convincing few seconds, I doubled back and headed for the exit.

When I caught up to Pam, she was waiting outside the store, her custom pink Sidekick already to her ear.

"But this is *huuge*—you have to come through." Pam held her lips in the pouty form of the last word she spoke. Judging from the soft tone of her voice, I could tell she was talking to Jake Tulagan, her boy-friend of ten months. By now the poor guy is used to Pam's overreacting. She treats everything like a five-alarm fire. I've tried to tell her about herself, but she insists it's in her genes. Not on her dad's Irish side, but her mom's Caribbean side.

"HDQ—Haitian Drama Queen—is embedded in my DNA," she likes to say.

Pam frowned as she eyed me and my jersey. *Whatever.* Volleyball jerseys are formfitting and cute—unlike the oversize basketball or football ones. But Pam is such a stylista, she wouldn't be caught sleeping in what I had on.

An Etsy devotee, my *gurl* is slowly turning her hobby—creating mash-up T-shirts from salvageable thrift store finds—into a small side business. But she gives me her funky designs for free. Even though I can't bring myself to wear them too often. They're just too *fabulous.* It's bad enough that I get the occasional once-over because of my long limbs, so I avoid wearing anything that might attract more head-to-toe eyeball scans.

"Thanks," she sighed into the phone. "See you there."

"What did you guilt him into this time?"

I teased as Pam tucked her cell into her half-moon-shaped bag.

"He promised to help me with my blog's redesign today, but now he's trying to push it to next week." She unraveled the chunky crocheted scarf from around her neck and tied it back on in a different style. "I can't be slackin' when that flashy copycat blog is trying to steal my shine."

As long as she's got creative blood pumping through her veins, Pam refuses to let her hip blog about local teen style get upstaged.

"I haven't seen you since your rubber ball assault." She put aside her redesign preoccupation and strolled in step with me. "How's work going?" Despite her HDQ leanings, Pam is a superthoughtful and caring person. Hers was the lone shoulder I leaned on in junior high when cold-blooded kids were calling me Elastigirl, thanks to my gangly arms and legs and bony body. It's hard to believe that just a few years later, natural hormones and high school volleyball teamed up to whip my physique into Venus Williams–esque form.

"I'll tell you the highlight of my morning," I continued, hoping my singsong voice piqued her curiosity. "This cu-TAY in *chief* got in my line when I was on register."

"Really, London?" Pam was touched, like I'd just handed her a bouquet of flowers. She couldn't hide her excitement over my interest in someone other than Unslick Rick. There was something about Rick that she hadn't liked from the get-go. Pam has a sixth sense for these things and she picked up on Rick's superficial stench almost immediately. He cared too much about appearances for Pam's taste. That's an ironic opinion coming from a fashion *gearu* like herself, but it's more about her disgust over his obsession with status.

Pam's theory is that Rick only hangs with people he's *expected* to hang out with. (This is unacceptable to a girl who learned at a tender age to ignore the stares her mixed-race family sometimes got when out in public.) Case in point: Last year, when Rick was a newbie freshman volleyballer, he started dating me, a fellow newbie volley-baller. As soon as Rick was crowned Peak Performance's Top Performer, he upgraded me for a star v-ball girlfriend. And ever since the incident, Pam *really* can't stand even talking about him.

I for one am grateful Pam doesn't care about status. She befriended me in my unpopular middle school days. And now that I've been branded the "jilted girl-friend," she's just as supportive.

"You should've seen your gurl acting all crazy, speeding through customers so Fly Guy could slide over to my faster line," I confessed. "I still don't know what got into me. It was like I *had* to meet him."

"What's his name?" she asked the minute we claimed an unoccupied bistro table outside our favorite sandwich shop.

I couldn't conjure a juicy response if I'd wanted to. My involuntary facial expressions—primarily acted out by my dark, thick eyebrows—always snitch my true feelings. My eyebrows twitched and rose, then in the next millisecond, lowered. This reflex babbled to Pam that this was the end of my crush story. Nothing else to say.

"Well, at least you now know there's crush life after Rick," she said before I could answer. "I'll go in and grab our lunch."

"Let me know if you need help carrying it out," I offered.

It had been only two weeks, but this was getting to be our Saturday-afternoon ritual.

And what made this ritual extra nice was finding a sweet lunch spot where we could people watch. For October it was a relatively warm day. Sitting in the sun would help us stay warm after we downed our cold soft drinks.

It was a great day for people watching. Lots of modely types were walking the Ave for some reason. The skater dudes hanging out near Starbucks were happy about that. Their jumps got riskier and more helter-skelter every time a group of girls walked by.

"It's mad busy out here," I commented as Pam and I ate. "I wonder what's going on today."

Sometimes, if the new bookstore was hosting an author signing, or if a performance at the arts center around the corner was poppin' off, there would be more foot traffic than usual. Pam shrugged and spotted someone interesting.

"He stays for*ever* framed out," she said of the guy walking by in white-rimmed shades. For the many times we'd run into him, we'd never seen his eyes—rain or shine. "Lookin' like Kanye West in that ole 'Stronger' video," Pam continued.

"I'm sayin'," I agreed.

"Ooooh, come with me to Cynthea Bey's store," Pam pleaded, as if in response to something she told herself in her mind. She checked the time on her cell phone. "I wanna see what she came up with for the winter season."

Cynthea Bey had opened Chic Boutique—a cool warehouse space showcasing local and popular designer labels—a little over two months ago. Pam, the Cynthea groupie, had visited almost every week. I think she was stalking so she could one day cross paths with the supermodel. Despite her unlucky timing, Pam continued to have hope.

"We've got twenty-five minutes before we have to be back," I warned Pam. She's an overscheduling freak if you don't rein her in.

She hadn't even swallowed all of her food, but she stood up and threw away the rest of her sandwich and baby carrots. If I wasn't such a fast eater and hadn't already been done with my turkey baguette, there's no way I would have been leaving with her.

By the time we turned the corner toward Chic Boutique, the sight of a long line snaking from the store to the sidewalk twisted our faces into WTF grimaces.

"Are they giving away free clothes or something? What's with that crazy long line?" I asked out loud, but more to myself than to Pam. The last thing I felt like doing was dealing with a bunch of maniacal girls all vying for the same size-four jeans.

Pam and I stood staring in a paralyzed pause, reading the large pink storefront sign's swirly letters: CASTING CALL TODAY: 15 JERSEY GIRLS WILL BE SELECTED TO COMPETE FOR THE CHANCE TO BECOME *THE* CHIC BOUTIQUE MODEL IN OUR IN-STORE PRINT ADS!

It was clear that Cynthea Bey was out to prove that New Jersey could bleed style like New York. *Good for her,* I thought.

"I've seen enough." I tried to snap Pam out of her daze. I could tell she was excited. Nothing this huge had happened in Teawood since the year before when Jay-Z and Beyoncé were spotted buying iced coffees at the corner café. "Let's get out of here. I'm starting to catch a Rachel Zoe–clone contact high." Pam didn't respond. "Quick, before I break out in an 'ohmygod' attack—or worse, break out in song." Still no response. "My humps. My humps. My lovely lady lumps."

Pam finally blinked; then she laughed

at my rendition. "I'm sorry, this must be torture for you. I'll come back when this all blows over."

That's when I saw him. The hottie customer from Art Attack was just a few yards from me. He was talking to girls in the outdoor casting line. Even though most guys would love to have been in his position, it didn't seem like he was trying to hit on anyone. Instead, he looked professional—snapping digital shots of each contestant, then attaching printed photos onto forms he collected from every girl.

"That's him, that's him!" I whisper-screamed. Pam knew right away what and whom I was talking about. She followed the direction of my gaze to the object of my obsess—er, affection.

He was as tall and calm as an oak tree. I wondered if that made me a pesky squirrel foraging for an acorn of his attention. It was nice to see him looking more relaxed than he had looked in Art Attack, where he'd gotten all bashful about coming up short. His former pocket-digging hands were now carrying a clipboard and a tiny camera. He pulled one of those cool portable photo printers from his back pocket.

The official-looking lanyard hanging around his neck confirmed that he wasn't loitering here to check out the girls. It also nicely topped off his intrepid reporter look. The only thing missing was a newsboy cap.

"What's he doing?" Pam asked.

Loverboy was holding his finger in the air, counting the heads of every girl in line outside. As he counted his way down and got closer to Pam and me, I was able to make out what was written in all caps on his lanyard: BRENT ST. JOHN, WWW.FACEMAG.COM, PHOTOGRAPHY INTERN.

That was when he reached us. He was mumbling numbers under his breath as he pointed at me and then finally Pam. "Twenty, twenty-one" I heard him say before he turned around and headed back to the first girl he had counted at the entrance of Chic Boutique. It seemed that there were also people standing inside the store who were being grouped in a separate head count.

"He thinks we're in line for this casting," I complained to Pam. *How did this happen?* I blamed it on the mesmerizing fuchsia storefront sign. We'd gotten caught up when we stood there frozen to read it.

Now our absentmindedness had made Fly Guy confused.

"This is a sign." A sudden gust of autumn wind blew Pam's flyaway strands into the sides of her mouth as she spoke excitedly. "You have to give him your number or something. Who knows if you'll ever meet him again? Much less twice in one day!"

He was about ten girls away from where we stood at the end of the line. I had to think fast. I had messed up the first time he and I were face-to-face. There had to be some way to strike up a conversation with him.

My inner scheming led me to the stack of applications jammed into a plastic brochure holder standing outside the store.

I grabbed one.

Pam knew where I was headed with this so she dug deep into her purse and furnished a pen. In the next hot minute, I was filling out the application as fast as I could.

Three

Name, age, address, phone number, e-mail.

Thank goodness there were no Miss America—esque questions about how to achieve world peace or anything. It was straightforward contact info and basic stats (height, eye and hair color, weight, etc.). I guessed Chic Boutique was making no bones about this search being based on looks.

This was the second time today that I was scrambling and rearranging circumstances to force a totally choreographed chance meeting with this guy. I'd never in my fifteen years been so impulsive about a boy. Rick was my first major boyfriend (if you don't count the hand-holding I used to do with my seventh-grade crush). There was no major excitement around Rick. We more or less started dating after hanging out at the same time (after school) and same place (Teawood High's auditorium) every other day. Our volleyballer friends overlapped and so we ended up chatting with each other. From there, our relationship progressed to texting and then to meeting up outside the school gym with our mutual friends. When we finally decided to meet up alone, we eased into a more defined relationship.

No major sparks or heart-stopping embraces. Rick and I had dug each other, but I'd felt nothing close to this unexplainable excitement that I seemed to feel around this stranger.

By the time the cutie was two girls away, I was done. My handwriting even had the appearance that I'd taken my time with the application. Best believe my phone number was especially clearly written—there was no way he would confuse my 7 for a 2 like other people usually did. If only I had a highlighter . . . or a tiny little airport ground crewman standing rigid on the page and waving tiny glow sticks toward the digits.

Beau Wow was within earshot now.

"Ohmygod, do you go to Warwick High?" an overenthusiastic girl asked him when he collected her application. "I swear you look familiar."

"Uh . . . yeah." House Special was caught off guard.

"Wait—aren't you in my Latin class?"

He simply nodded yes, obviously hoping to signal that he wasn't in the mood for chitchat. It was crystal clear that this was the first conversation this girl had ever had with him. Classic case of popular student finally talks to unnoticed classmate when it's in her best interest to do so. As much as His Royal Hotness stood out to me, I could see how the popular set might pass Luscious over as a nobody. He was somewhat shy instead of showy; he gave off an intense vibe, instead of a self-absorbed one; and he had a certain sensitivity rather than a swagger.

"So you're like a fashion photographer or something?" She shot him a vote-for-me grin like she expected her photo printout to be pressed into a campaign button.

Lawd, make her stop. I was getting annoyed by her fake conversation attempt, but Cutie handled the inquisition with understated tact. He just half smiled in response and then thanked her for her application and moved to the next person in line.

The popular girl didn't seem to know what to make of his reaction. I think it was confusing to her that she didn't get a rise— pun intended—out of a boy. Especially a boy from the lower end of the social totem pole.

I liked him even more. He just went through the motions of his duties without missing a step in his work rhythm.

"Thanks," he said as he collected the application from a brunette with a pixie haircut. He scanned the application to make sure it was correctly filled out and then pointed his tiny silver camera at Pixie. She immediately gave him a bored-with-life supermodel look and he snapped. In the next few seconds, a mechanical sound whirred as the printer pushed out a slim photograph of the aspiring model. Future Boyfriend pulled a thin sheet of waxed paper off the back of the self-adhesive photo and stuck the picture to the application. As the girl asked him an inaudible question, she pushed her ankles out and nervously balanced on the outsides of her feet.

"You'll hear from the judges by tomorrow if you've been selected," he told her.

She quietly thanked him and then exited the line.

As soon as he moved on to the next girl, a sleek black sports car pulled up in front of Chic Boutique. When the passenger door opened, a long, elegant leg emerged. The car was like a suave brotha, and the sexy leg a toothpick teetering out the side of his mouth. From where we were standing, the deeply tinted windows blocked our view of the person attached to the leg. But by the sound of the hushed gasps, we knew it was Cynthea Bey. Pam quietly sucked in air.

"Ohmygod," she said in one released breath.

"See?" I teased her, hoping to thwart an HDQ episode. "Being here has already exposed you to the 'OMG' virus, and I have no antidote."

The bad joke fell on deaf ears. But I didn't have to think of a funnier one. Pam kept her composure, which is totally uncharacteristic. I took this to mean she was more excited than I'd ever seen her. Pam simply turned to me and said in a measured voice, "I won't be able to live with myself if I don't try to score an interview with her for my blog."

We watched Cynthea Bey emerge from the car, looking stunning in a rust-colored wrap dress and the most exquisite pair of leather flats I'd ever seen. Her hair was pulled away from her face into a low bun. The large dark eyes that have earned her the title of "doe-eyed darling of the runway" looked even larger in real life. Now we could see firsthand why she's known as the girl next door gone international glam. She was not unrealistically gorgeous, nor did she have an edgy beauty. She was simply pretty. Pretty like a two-dimensional cartoon in a Disney movie. In fact, she did kind of resemble Jasmine from the classic *Aladdin*.

Before stepping away from the car, Cynthea leaned over and thanked the shadowy figure of a driver. As the sexy car pulled away, the stretched reflections of Teawood's neat row of brick storefronts glided across the car's black windows. Two Chic Boutique employees had rushed out to greet Ms. Bey. As they ushered her toward the store, they briefed her on how the casting was going. Cynthea paused and flashed her million-dollar smile to all the model wannabes grouped outside.

"Hello, lovelies!" she generously offered

to everyone—including to Pam and me, who were back to our staring paralysis. Cynthea continued greeting people as she stepped inside her store.

Pam corrected her posture and faced Chic Boutique's entrance like a style soldier reporting for fashion duty. She stood still for a second, took a slow, deep breath, and then announced, "Be right back."

I was thrilled for Pam, but forgot to wish her good luck because the selfish part of me was too concerned that I now had to face my crush alone. Without Pam's easy, ice-breaking conversational skills to lean on.

All the action that was paused while everyone studied Cynthea's grand entrance kicked back into gear. The cutie snapped a photo of the girl in front of me and attached it to her application. *Here he comes,* I thought.

"Hi," he said politely. "Your application, please."

I handed it to him without saying a word. He started reviewing what I'd written down. It didn't seem like he remembered me. I guess I looked different without my Art Attack vest on. Not to mention, I was no longer wearing the checkout counter around my waist.

I had to think fast if I was going to make an impression. Like, *quick*. As soon as he reached for the camera, our face-to-face time would almost be over. *It's now or never, gurl. Say something.*

"Don't worry about the two dollars you owe me," I blurted out.

I had hoped this would jog his memory as to who I was, but judging from the crazy amount of creases my statement etched on his forehead, he didn't take it that way.

"Look," he said, before looking around to make sure no one overheard what I'd said. "Thank you for what you did for me. I really appreciate it. But I don't have any pull with the judges, so I can't help you."

Before I could protest, he pointed the camera at me. Not willing to screw things up any more than I already had, I didn't refuse his picture. With the last bit of dignity I had left, I looked at the camera but couldn't bring myself to smile. He snapped anyway.

"Thank you," he said, searching my application before adding " . . . London."

He looked up from his photo-printing drill and caught me staring. I was busted, but I couldn't look away. His dark brown eyes unexpectedly locked with mine. My right eyebrow reacted to his intense gaze with a subtle twitch. As usual, I couldn't stop my facial expression from squealing that I'm a total fan. We stayed like this for only about three seconds. But, honestly, it felt more like ONE-file-a-chipped-nail-TWO-and-another-nail-THREE than ONE-Mississippi-TWO-Mississippi-THREE.

I had been watching him from ten girls ago and he hadn't offered any personal touches or lingered in his encounters with any of them. Maybe this meant something.

"Thank you," I said, taking an obvious glance at his name tag, before continuing, ". . . Brent."

I saw his Adam's apple rise, then fall, like he'd just swallowed. I stretched my lips into a slight smile, and then we both moved on in opposite directions—he to the cell-phone-chatting girl behind me in line, and I to hunt down Pam inside the store.

Running would be too dorky so I decided against it. The urge was strong because mini good news like this is something you want to share fast. Any delay in telling Pam every single detail about my heart-pounding moment with Brent would fall too short of satisfaction. I had to tell her while the subtle, flirtatious exchanges were fresh in my mind. It felt like it was my birthday and I wanted Pam to watch me blow out the candles before melted globs of Crayola-colored wax ruined my designer cake. Reviewing the details in my head while rushing into the store was like protecting my imaginary cake's dancing flames from the wind my speed walking generated.

But before I could locate her, I smacked right into what can only be described as door chimes in human form. My collision with a boho-chic chick in oversize shades caused the numerous metal bracelets on her arms to jangle in surround sound. I was too distracted by the clanging of the jewelry to notice who I'd just bumped into.

"London?" The girl recognized me after we'd pulled apart and muttered apologies. "What are *you* doing *here*?"

When she (loudly) took off her sunglasses, I realized who it was. *Oh, great.* I almost let out an exasperated sigh. *Kelly Fletcher, my childhood frenemy.*

Her unflattering question was meant to make me feel like a mutt at the Westminster dog show.

Kelly was the last person I wanted to run into while on a natural high. Her presence alone is a buzz kill. Seeing Kelly at that moment was like having a power outage in the middle of my highest-scoring Guitar Hero session on record. It's not because she's a mean person or anything. It's just what the girl represents to me. The mere sight of her opens the floodgates of embarrassing childhood memories.

Kelly and I have known each other since toddlerhood. Our moms used to be "friends"—if you can use that word to describe two competitive mothers who used their daughters' achievements to one-up each other.

Our moms were part of the child-actor circuit in Manhattan. We all met at a kiddie casting for a department store's fall catalog. Because the two of them were from the same Jersey town, the women struck up a fellowship and promised to keep each other informed about casting news that came down the Manhattan grapevine.

Hard to imagine, but yes. Mom was once rapt by my looks.

My mother had a few good years of heaven on earth, getting showered with compliments about her darling daughter. Tons of old photos of me commemorate that bygone era. I know it's not my fault, but I still feel weirdly responsible about the way things turned out. Before I hit middle school, my once cherubic, heart-shaped face started stretching longer and longer as I grew taller and lankier. By the eighth grade, that oblong face was practically covered with zits. It was a good thing my dermatologist mother had access to all the zit-zappin' skin-care products or there would've been no hope for me.

Kelly, meanwhile, had no such misfortune. Puberty granted her more beauty wishes than a fairy godmother. But far be it from me to hate.

Awkward history aside, every time we cross paths, Kelly and I are cordial.

"I was just heading in to find my friend," I half-truthed. "You?"

"My agent sent me down for this casting," she told me with a straight face. I should've known that she would take up modeling professionally. In an imperfect world, the haves keep on having. Pretty soon I'd be seeing her face on those giant billboards over the Manhattan-bound entrance of the Lincoln Tunnel.

Kelly smirked and then, without realizing it, flipped her wavy mane of glossy brown hair like she was shooting a Pantene commercial. "Yeah, right. I barely even know of a *travel* agent," she added sarcastically. I panicked for a moment, wondering if I'd thought aloud and she'd heard. "On the bright side—no agent means there's no one to stop my mom from running things her way."

"She's still hoping to get you on the cover of *Vogue*, huh?" I sympathized.

"You know it," Kelly admitted. "And is your mom still hoping the same for you?" She flipped the tables yet again. "Is that why you signed up?"

"Yes and no." I kept it simple. Getting tricked into believing that Kelly and I aren't frenemies was not going to work on me. Heart-to-heart chat or not. "What about you?" I tossed back, running the same game.

"Same here," she said. "I actually want to pursue modeling and acting, so this is a good prep for the real opportunities. It'll be fun."

She was talking as if she had already been selected to be the face of Chic Boutique. I guess she figured that if her competition was a girl like me, she had it in the bag. *Go 'head, gurl, with your confident self,* I fake cheered after Kelly and I offered each other good luck and moved on. Some people just roll through town like they're perched on top of a parade float!

Suddenly, I looked around and asked myself what I was doing among groups of stylistas who looked like the *Deal or No Deal* suitcase models. I wasn't fooling anyone— least of all myself. This wasn't my type of crowd. With the hot intern encounter out of the way, there was no other reason for me to stick around. It was time to find Pam and get us away from this scene.

I found her near the fitting rooms in the back of the store. Her copper-colored hair was the easiest marker—especially since she was wearing it out in all its cotton candy

beaming!" I didn't

until we rounded the corner at the Starbucks that we started squealing.

Our shriek fest helped the flirty madness of the last twenty minutes rush back to me and I found it all so crazy funny.

"I have never done something so wildly impulsive in all my life!" I shouted.

"Me too!" She exhaled. "But let me tell you what happened. Wait—no, you first."

"No, you first. There's nothing really to tell except that *Brent* and I had a moment."

"Brent? Oh, it's like *that*?"

"That don't mean nothing 'cept I can read." I downplayed the encounter. It was best not to get Pam thinking I had a chance with this guy. She'd nag me about it until I regretted making up too much backstory. "I wanna know if you replaced my true-blue friendship for Cynthea Bey's."

"I would trade your true-blue fri

The next afternoon when my cell phone rang, I didn't think anything of it when I didn't recognize the number on the caller ID. To save money on her limited cell-phone-minutes plan, Pam often calls me from any landline she can use. If it's during peak hours, she'll even borrow her mom's cell phone if it can save her a buck. After getting slapped with a three-hundred-dollar cell phone bill two months ago, Pam hasn't been cutting down on the amount of gabbing she does on the phone. She's been cutting down on the gabbing she does on her *cell* phone. The girl will still find a way to call and report the slightest news she hears.

"Hello," I answered a bit breathlessly because I'd just finished flinging a pillow at my keeps-sneaking-into-my-room-when-I'm-not-home brother Wyatt.

"Hi, is this London?" asked an older woman with a posh British accent.

"Yes." I still didn't have a clue who I was speaking to.

"London, this is Asha Kumar of the Chic Boutique Model Search. You have been selected as one of our finalists in the modeling contest."

My overactive imagination pressed play

on the daydream reel starring Phine Photographer. It's the one about him wanting to see me again so badly, he digitally doctored my image (i.e., erased the flyaway hair strands, shaped my eyebrows, gave my skin a clear glow), and took a Polaroid of it.

"Really?" I asked, my voice loaded with vitamin C for cynicism.

I wondered if I should play along. When she first started talking, I almost thought she was really someone else. *The girl is good*, I thought with a smile.

"Pam?" I called out as I leaned over and rested my free hand on my knee the way my grandma does when she's trying to stop herself from laughing before getting to the punch line. "You big Keira *Not*-ly, *Fake*-omi Campbell, Kate *Loss* wannabe British joker. I should've known this was you!"

The silence on the other end wasn't feeling too golden. I immediately thought of that cell-phone commercial where the call drops just after someone says something funny but borderline offensive. Just like the commercial, I wasn't sure how my caller was taking my playful response.

"Ms. Abrams, I can assure you this is no joke." The sophistication in the woman's voice was unruffled, but I could tell it now carried a hint of disapproval in it, thanks to my unclassy reaction.

"I—I'm sorry," I offered feebly, my heart pounding in my ear.

"You are one of fifteen girls selected to participate in a five-week modeling contest," she started without missing a beat. "As you probably already know, *Face* is an e-zine today, but for decades we were a print magazine and Cynthea Bey was one of our treasured cover girls."

I held the receiver inches from my mouth so the sound of my heavy breathing would go undetected.

"Well, this contest will unfold entirely on Facemag.com," the woman continued. "Our readers will get to vote on which three contestants will be eliminated each week. On Saturday at nine thirty a.m., all fifteen contestants are to report to Chic Boutique. We'll need everyone to stay for at least two hours. Can you make it?"

Despite my earlier unprofessionalism—which she had ignored—she sounded all business.

"Yes," I heard myself answer, even though I wasn't available. I had to be at work at nine thirty that morning. But after my initial ghetto response, I had to show this woman that I wasn't as hood as my first impression made me out to be. "Uh, sorry about earlier. I hadn't expected a callback."

"Well, I don't see why. We found your look especially alluring. In our book, that's worthy of a callback."

Alluring? I didn't know how to respond to that. I hadn't even bothered to properly comb my hair that day. Plus, I didn't trust myself to screw this up by saying anything else.

"Hah," I forced out of my throat in a well-how-about-that tone.

"Wonderful, Miss Abrams." Her back-to-business phone manner still sounded like a caricature of itself. "I will meet you then."

By the time I hung up, I was sure that this hadn't been a joke. Still, from the sheer randomness of it all, I couldn't help chuckling.

Four

"Just give me a second to let it sink in," Pam requested. She let her body fall backward onto the mountain of pillows lining my bed. She had rushed over as soon as I texted her with the news. It had been only seven minutes since the stoic British caller's unexpected phone call.

When she was through staring at the ceiling fan, she asked me to take it from the top and retell the phone conversation for the umpteenth time. I obliged.

"A-*llur*-ring." Pam let the word balance on the tip of her tongue like a pirouetting ballerina.

"Don't get hung up on that description." I plopped down on the sunlit window seat.

I was tired of pacing. "It's super noncommittal. It can mean everything and nothing much."

"What are you, crazy?" She sat up like she'd regained her energy. "I don't know if you're fishing for compliments, but don't let me run through all your fly features. Starting with your prominent cheek bones, your graceful long neck and fit body. Matter of fact, I'd compare you to Jourdan Dunn— that model who was rippin' the runway all New York Fashion Week."

"*Hiiiii*, Pam." My brother Wyatt moseyed on into my room dressed like he just raided Ne-Yo's gentleman's closet.

"Get *out*!" I pointed to the door. Ever since Wyatt turned twelve, he had started believing he could actually woo girls.

"Catch you later." He spun around like he had on Heelys and strolled on out with serious swagger.

We both busted out laughing when the door closed behind him. I secretly wished I had as much resilience after a public rejection.

"Anyway, Pam. You forget who you're talking to." I attempted to mask my uneasiness with accepting compliments. "The only reason I know as much as I do about Cynthea Bey is because she's a hometown girl. I wouldn't know Jourdan Dunn from the latest pair of Jordan sneakers."

Okay, so that last comment went a little overboard. I didn't want Pam to think I was a complete ingrate.

"But thanks, Pammie. You're right— I'm gonna walk in there on Saturday and act like I know. It's about me checking out something different."

"Yeah, whatever." Pam was also ready to shift from the mushy moment. "You just wanna go in to check out what Brent is all about."

"You ain't *nevah* lie!"

I ducked as she threw a 2004 USA Volleyball Team commemorative pillow at me.

"You know what this means?" Mom asked me excitedly when I handed her the contest consent forms to sign. She twisted in her home office swivel chair to face me. "All that volleyball put you in great shape to do some modeling. I guess it wasn't a bad thing after all!"

"It was never a bad thing." My words

were peppered with a little attitude. I couldn't help it. The woman confuses me sometimes. She's the first one to brag about my v-ball games to relatives, yet she'd rather I be into some other extracurricular activity. "And that's not why I picked up volleyball," I reminded her.

My mom didn't need reminding about why I loved it. She was the one who first introduced me to the sport. I had just turned ten when the 2004 summer Olympics was in full swing. Prikeba "Keba" Phipps was on the USA's women's team. I was mesmerized watching all the extending of long limbs over the net with powerhouse moves that honored the women's statuesque build.

"You see what tall girls like you can do?" My mom's voice was as comforting as her arm around me. It had been an awful day. During my summer camp trip to the Bronx Zoo, I'd overheard a group of kids crackin' that I must've escaped from the giraffe enclosure. By the time I got home, I was crying my eyes out, blaming my mom for letting me leave the house wearing my favorite embroidered jean shorts. That was the day my adoration with shorts temporarily ended. I didn't like the way they exposed my legs to ridicule. Years later, of course, I proudly rock my tiny volleyball shorts on the court.

Since Giraffegate, I stopped slouching (for height-shrinkage effect) and started collecting a growing mental list of famous tall women—height five ten and higher—for inspiration. Today that list of nonmodels/nonballers includes gospel singer Yolanda Adams, Taylor Swift, Jordin Sparks, comedienne Aisha Tyler, TV chef Padma Lakshmi, girl golfer Michelle Wie, Queen Latifah, Mandy Moore, and First Lady Michelle Obama.

"Aren't you even gonna read the small print?" I watched, incredulous, as she happily scribbled her signature across the bottom of the form.

"This is the best news," she said, ignoring me. "I always hoped you would be a part of something like this. You always were a natural."

I'm a natural at volleyball, my inner brat hissed, giving her a raspberry.

I didn't bother bringing up my struggle to raise the sports-camp fee. It wouldn't do me any good. My parents rarely renege on their decisions. It's a policy they say started after the twins were born. I've heard the story a million times. Warren and Wyatt's presence turned their smooth-sailing household into pure pandemonium and I've seen the pictures that prove it. (My favorite is the one of Mom unwittingly wearing two different kinds of shoes on her feet while out at the park. Talk about *out* of it.) And word is, that crazy era nearly split up Mom and Dad. The type-A personalities that they are— especially in my dad's case—led my parents to crack down on the chaos by planning way ahead and sticking to those plans. So when my junior high school coach recommended I try for the Peak Performance program the summer *after* junior year, my parents locked that in their minds.

Seeing her grinning from ear to ear over this modeling contest was so frustrating. I was almost positive that if I'd asked, my mom would have dropped a grand on this modeling contest before you could say, "Sashay, Chanté." Somewhere inside, my emotional microwave popcorn bag was getting nuked on a revolving tray.

The following Saturday at 9:15 a.m., I took a deep breath before entering Chic Boutique. Pam had convinced me not to dress like a screaming sports fan in the nose-bleed seats. So for the first time this season, I benched my MVP—the v-ball jersey—and wore one of Pam's signature T-shirts as a sub.

When Pam told me she designed this particular T with me in mind, I had to ask her if she'd ever met me. It's nothing like my style. Off the shoulder on one side, it makes me look more muscular than I am. But I had to admit that the blue skinny jeans and tribal-print Old Navy flats that Pam had me rock made the outfit look extra cute.

My hair was pulled back in a high bun, as always. But a satin head scarf added a chicer accent than the wide black bands I usually go with.

Chic Boutique had a different look after hours. The center clothing fixtures had been pushed off to either side of the area in front of the expansive white checkout counter, creating a clearing sizable enough to have a dance-off in. Three tall bar stools positioned behind the counter faced this clearing. A few thin manila folders and pens were neatly lined up in front of each chair.

I hope this is worth missing work today, I thought. Goth Guy hooked me up by taking my morning Art Attack shift. He was happy to do it because he said he owed me one. (Eager to pick up some extra cash, I'd volunteered to cover his early evening shift a few days prior.) I wasn't expected to report to work until much later that afternoon.

These days, I welcomed any opportunity to earn extra money for my summer camp. The fifteen-hundred-dollar fee was due in like three months and I only had three hundred saved. I needed all the overtime and extra hours I could get. Crushing on someone new (and feeling excited about it!) couldn't be a more fun distraction from all this financial pressure. I wondered when/if Loverboy would make an appearance.

The contestants trickled in. I recognized a couple of them from casting day—like the Miss Popularity who fired off a million and one questions at Brent. Some of the girls carried leather portfolios with them. I suddenly felt unprepared. What if the British caller was so unimpressed with my reaction to her that she opted not to tell me to bring photos. Not that I have any professional photos of myself. But those JPEGs of me wearing Pam's shirt designs for her blog are better than nothing.

I noticed the girl with the pixie haircut.

She was the only one who I felt comfortable talking to at this point. Awkwardly lurking around the sweater-dress fixture, she seemed approachable and more down-to-earth than the others.

"Excuse me." I lightly tapped her on the arm and she turned to face me. "Hi." I introduced myself. "I'm London."

"I'm Maya." She smiled slightly.

"Hi, Maya. I was wondering if we were supposed to bring anything along with us today. Like photos?"

"No, not that I know of." Her eyes scanned the black portfolios that three girls were cradling in their arms. "I was just told to be here at nine thirty and expect to stay for about two hours."

Whew, I thought. *That sounds about right.*

"Thanks," I told her and meant it. Her normalness was reassuring, and I felt like I had company there even though that was all we said to each other for the rest of the morning.

Oddly, I calmed down a bit and scolded myself for getting so caught up in the first place. After all, this contest wasn't a huge deal. I had to remind myself of the time I performed like a champ on the volleyball court in front of a crowd of five hundred. I'm used to being in the mix and I rise to the occasion when it's called for. How could I now let a fluffy competition like this take me off my game? Besides, I came only because I was curious about what this was all about. I wanted to find out if this was one big practical joke, or if they really were interested in me.

When I'd counted that thirteen girls (including myself) were present, a rail-thin woman in black skinny jeans and a black beaded tunic appeared from the stock room. Her dark brown hair was pulled back into a sleek ponytail and her plum lipstick blended nicely with her suntanned skin. She was followed by a man in brown horn-rimmed glasses and a crew cut, wearing a white T-shirt and a red checkered hipster head scarf around his neck. He looked like a gay rock star. I immediately decided to be his best friend if Pam ever ditched me for Cynthea Bey. Or even if she didn't. And assuming he'd have me as a BFF.

The fierce-looking woman in black was the first to speak.

"We're just waiting on one more judge and the rest of the contestants to join us," she announced. My stomach did flip-flops when I recognized her voice. It was the British caller.

The man whispered something in her ear and they both chuckled and kicked off a conversation.

I heard the clickety clack of heels rushing to the scene. The final two contestants were arriving with only but a minute to spare before the 9:30 a.m. call time. Typical diva behavior. I had the feeling this was a tactical move to get all eyes on them as they walked in. That's why I didn't look. Maya fell for it hard. She turned her head in their direction and I watched as her eyes lingered and rolled up and down their bodies.

Hmm, I thought. *They must have some attention-grabbing gear on 'cause Pixie can't look away.* I couldn't tell what her exact reaction was, but it was clear that they were interesting to look at.

British Caller and Gay Rock Star were drawn to the latecomers as well. British Caller nodded at them as if to signal that she was impressed with their getups. I still refused to give them the satisfaction of looking their way.

In the next second, the third judge arrived. She looked like an aging Kate Moss.

She was hauling a handbag that was about half her size. It hinged on her bent elbow and slapped against her midriff with each long stride to the center counter.

The other two judges took their positions, each perched high on a bar stool behind the counter. Equally fabulous official expressions formed on their faces. If this were a TV reality show, some dramatic, moment-of-truth music would be edited in at this point.

"Welcome, ladies," Mr. Rock Star bellowed like a stage actor and made eye contact with each of us. "My name is Didier Martineau and I'm the art director of what I'm sure is your favorite online fashion magazine, Facemag.com." His charisma pulled a shy smile out of most of the nervous girls. He spoke like a local until he said his name—which he pronounced with a spectacular French accent, with extra emphasis on the throaty *r*'s. "Welcome, one and all."

"I believe I met most of you over the phone," British Caller spoke next, pausing to peer at me and point her sharp chin in my direction. I wanted to throw one of the fixture's coats over my head. "I'm Asha Kumar, editor in chief of Facemag.com. Didier and

I are thrilled to be here for this, the first of what promises to be an annual model search for Chic Boutique. Facemag.com has partnered with Cynthea, a three-time *Face* cover girl. This is our way of continuing that partnership and collaborating on something we both feel strongly about: the next generation of fashion icons. All fifteen of you have been selected because of your individuality and singular appeal. We ask that you seriously consider if this contest is a journey you want to fully take on, because you are expected to stick with it unless dismissed either by online reader votes or the panel."

I was surprised that this was going to be such a huge event and not just about the store's grand opening. *How the heck did a simple, spur-of-the-moment ploy to get noticed by a boy land me here?* I wondered with (slightly amused) bewilderment. They were giving me an easy out, but my curiosity was keeping my feet glued to the shiny boutique floor. In my head I sketched out a pros and cons chart. At the top of the pros column, I mentally scribbled *Brent the Babe*. Under that, I listed *Doing something different*. And, as much as I hated to admit it, somewhere on that column was *The deep satisfaction of knowing Rick will kick himself when he realizes he unceremoniously dumped a modeling contestant with "singular appeal."* Of course, on the flip side, the number one con weighed as much as every pro put together. *Fulfilling Mom's wish for a "model" daughter* definitely could make this feel less enjoyable. Another huge negative was the toll that a huge commitment like this would have on my work, school, and volleyball schedules.

Despite all my inner arguments, I didn't budge. The room was too jam-packed with tension. Looking as enthused as front-row VIPs at a haute couture fashion show, the fashionista panel was frozen in silence and wearing bored-with-life expressions. They stared at everyone for a few moments longer. I was glad when someone finally spoke.

"I guess that leaves me." The giggly third judge must've had one too many mimosas that morning. The girls laughed uncomfortably at her attempted joke. "I'm Monica Lester and I represent Bey Modeling Agency. Cynthea's two-year-old agency has had much success in its short life. Now I'm proud to offer my insight into this modeling contest. You, darling ladies, will be judged on five key qualities found in both our valued Chic

Boutique shopper and a professional model of Cynthea's caliber—your presentation, professionalism, talent, personal style, and confidence. At the end of each of the contest's first four weeks, three of you will be eliminated by online reader votes. In the fifth and final week, the winner, chosen by this panel of judges, will be the face of our spring campaign and the recipient of a one-year modeling contract with Bey Agency. And . . ." She paused to wink at us. "Watch this space for news of special gifts to be awarded to other worthy contestants."

"Any questions?" Asha looked around the room and her gaze landed at the back, where the latecomers had settled. "Yes, and can you please give us your name before you ask your question, so we can get the introductions started?"

"Hi," I heard the voice say. I knew it immediately. My heart rate quickened. "My name is Kelly Fletcher. I was just wondering, what inspired Cynthea to launch this contest?"

This ain't no press conference, I thought. *Katie Couric called—she wants her interview questions back.* Just trying to earn bonus points as usual. I stole a glance at Kelly, which didn't help me feel any better. First of all, the girl was decked out like she'd swagger-jacked Rihanna. It was as if a professional stylist hooked up her outfit. A cropped biker-chick jacket, gray flouncy miniskirt, black tights, a killer pair of ankle boots, and accessories galore. Her long brown hair was bent into large curls so she looked even more Vanessa Hudgens–esque than usual.

"That's an excellent question," a clearly impressed Asha responded. "This has always been a dream of Cynthea's. As you all know, she's a hometown girl and was raised just a few blocks away from this very spot. The people and places that inspired her are all around her and she wants to give thanks to Teawood and this whole county and state by offering one of Jersey's own a chance at success in the fashion industry."

Asha paused in case there was a follow-up question. Her triangular face was poised like a pampered kitten. Asking questions and engaging her in discussion seemed to be the way to win her favor. She reminded me of the type of person Oprah would invite on as a guest, someone whose enthusiasm for her job was palpable. Like Cesar Millan the Dog Whisperer or Lisa Ling the intrepid global reporter. Asha loved what she did for a living, I could see that now.

"If there are no other questions, let's have the rest of you introduce yourselves, please." Her smile was genuine.

"It's my pleasure to finally meet you. I've read a lot about you and I've enjoyed your writing for years." The girl next to Kelly finally took a breath. I felt embarrassed for her because she squeaked as if someone squeezed her tummy, Kewpie-doll-style, to force air and words out of her mouth. That's how excited about the contest she was. She had been bobbing her head while talking as if she were being manipulated by an invisible puppeteer hand resting in the back of her head.

The next person was encouraged to say a few words. And then the next. By the time I was next to speak, I had to muster the courage not to run out of the boutique. Everyone was gorgeous, polished, and fashion conscious. And it was increasingly obvious that I was selected as the token jock of the bunch. They let me in to tip the beauty scale. Apparently, one of me must bring enough averageness to balance out fourteen stunning girls.

I was cut off before I even uttered a word. The disruption of a group of heavy walkers carrying clanking equipment snapped everyone off their focus.

Rock Star Didier stretched his torso and peered over our heads to get a clear view of the interrupters.

"Just one moment while I have a word with my photography crew." Didier held up his finger, signaling for me to hold my thought.

Now would be a good time to make for the exit, I thought. A redheaded man with a shoulder bag of equipment greeted the panel and then began speaking to Didier in hushed tones. Three people tagged behind that man and politely waited a respectful distance away on the sidelines for the conversation to be over. I suspected who one of those three people was. I had a sudden strong feeling in my bones that I was being watched.

My eyes led me to the person examining me with Superman-like vision. Brent St. John, photography intern, didn't seem to mind that he was caught staring. He looked right back at me. I was the first to look away.

If there had been a look of deep yearning and flaming desire in his eyes, maybe I would've held his gaze. But his watchfulness was simply observant—in the least romantic way possible. If he were the whistling type, right at that moment, he'd blow out a whistle-while-you-work ditty rather than a construction-site-catcall whistle. His look was more *Hunh, she made the final fifteen*, than *Yes, we meet again*.

If only the exit could have crept to *me*. That way, one nonchalant side step would have gotten me outta there unnoticed.

"Next, please." Didier was finished chatting with the head photographer and looked at me expectantly. "Let's continue the intros with the alluring mademoiselle with the fabulous hair."

I almost turned around to see who he was talking about.

"My name is London Abrams" I heard myself say. "I was born and raised in Teawood, and I never thought much about how special or cool that was until Cynthea Bey started highlighting all the good this community does. Now I feel more proud of my hometown and of its people."

There was a long silence after I said the last word. Everyone thought that my sentence would come to a more obviously definitive end, so they gave me time to complete my thought. But that was all I had to say. I didn't know how to wrap things up in a more full-stop way. Maybe they expected me to end with a high-pitched whoop like kids on that old *TRL* show. My fantasy best friend Didier was the first to realize that I was done speaking.

"Thank you, *Londres*," he said, translating my name into French. For all the comments, questions, and wisecracks that name has brought me ("I see London, I see France . . ."), I'd never had anyone come up with that one. That was mad hot. I wouldn't mind being called *Londres*. If I ever became an eccentric musician like Björk or became, like, the female ODB, I would straight-up change my name to that. No doubt.

Once introductions were out of the way, the photographers began setting up their equipment and the judges placed us in five groups of three.

"Now, let's see what you're all about, ladies." All the humor of her initial intro was lost from judge Monica's voice. She had switched into work mode and ditched the pleasantries. "We don't expect cover girl quality photos today. Just experiment and become familiar with having a professional camera pointed at you. These shots are for your online bio."

Monica called out the names of three girls and asked the rest of us to follow Asha to a break room in the back of the store.

The three girls looked a bit confused. I knew how they felt. I wasn't sure if my group was lucky not to be chosen or if that trio lucked out by getting their photo shoot over with first.

The rest of us walked through an employees-only door and down a narrow hallway to an open area where a long table and fold-up chairs were flanked by vending machines and a large white refrigerator.

"Please grab a seat and make yourselves comfortable," Asha said and began handing out questionnaires for us to fill out during the wait. "Be honest in your answers. And remember to let your personalities shine through. Be as deep, funny, witty, or dramatic as you'd like. This will be our readers' introduction to you."

As dramatic as I want? I thought. *How's this for drama? I don't belong in this contest. I feel like this is a huge mistake.*

The only time I looked up from my paper was when I reached for a pen in the center of the table. Sitting next to the contestants made me feel inadequate as it was. I didn't need reminders of how much more fly their look was.

A few minutes later, three of us were led to the small set of the photo shoot. Brent was nowhere to be found. Just my luck that he was assisting the photographer working on a separate group of girls. I felt gypped. I skipped work for nothing.

"London, you first," Asha announced.

I get the feeling she doesn't like me, I inwardly sulked. But dutifully I parked myself on the bar stool planted in front of the white canvas background. The two other girls in my group watched from the sidelines, ready to learn from my mistakes.

Not knowing what else to do, I looked straight into the lens, tilted my head to the right, and smiled.

The photographer had barely snapped two shots of me in this pose when Asha interrupted. "This isn't a yearbook picture, ladies. Be expressive, and show some energy and personality."

This was embarrassing. I didn't know

whether I should frame my face with my hands or growl like Catwoman.

Help came in the form of something unexpected. The moment the photo intern turned on a small wind machine in the corner of the set, my inner Naomi Campbell showed up. (I didn't even know I *had* one of those!) Something about being in the spotlight while feeling that breeze on my face and through my hair was exhilarating. Suddenly I discovered that I was on a swivel seat. I swung around. My back to the camera, I turned my head and looked piercingly into the lens. Next, I secured one foot on the floor and rotated my body so that I could rock some profile swag.

Ciara's "Click Flash" started playing in my head. I guess Beyoncé videos were unofficial modeling tutorials because I was totally diva channeling.

"Nice!" the photographer repeated between flashes. "Looking good."

What was surprising to me was that that's exactly how I felt.

Time may heal wounds, but it also has a way of chipping away at your confidence. I left the shoot riding high off that feeling you get after you've just aced an exam. But within a few hours, doubt settled in. I got to wondering if all that pose striking had struck the wrong chord. And as much as I said it to myself, my "what's done is done" mantra didn't chase away that nervous energy.

Volleyball turned out to be the best antidote for my lost mojo. I headed home and practiced some power serves and spikes against the unfinished basement wall until my head cleared.

Later that evening I forced myself to take a peak at Face's site. I told myself I'd only skim through the contest post and check out everyone's head shots and questionnaire answers. I started out feeling curious and ended up being pleasantly surprised.

Is that me? I hardly recognized myself. A different side of me came out in the photos. I actually looked *modelly*.

The reader votes were in. My approval rating was high enough to save me from the bottom three (I placed twelfth).

Not bad for a token jock.

Five

I saw the e-mail before I heard the voice mail.

The computer-generated message in my inbox from Facemag.com simply listed one thing. *His* name: Brent St. John.

Giddy with anticipation, I listened to the message on my cell phone. It had been turned off during the Sunday matinee movie I took in with the fam.

"Hello, London, congratulations on placing in the top twelve of Chic Boutique's Face of Spring competition. Now onto the next challenge," contest judge Asha Kumar's recorded drone began. "A shadow photographer has been assigned to each contestant. On one unspecified day this week, that photographer will pay you a surprise visit and document what you routinely do. In the next hour, look out for the e-mail naming who *your* shadow photographer will be. Good luck!"

I replayed the entire message a few times more.

Brent St. John had been named my shadow photographer. *Shadow photographer!* That meant that he would have to follow *me* around. I couldn't believe how this was all playing right into my hands. I felt like a villain in one of those retro Boomerang cartoons. All I needed was a signature maniacal laugh.

Come Monday morning, I woke up early and spent close to an hour getting my outfit game-tight. The open-sleeved, flowy top tucked into my booty-enhancing pair of boyfriend-fit cords worked the right look without trying too hard.

At school I freshened up my lip gloss on my way to each class just in case Brent popped out from behind a locker or underneath a staircase.

When the last period of the day came and went without a sign of Brent, I didn't think too much of it. Sure, I'd gotten dressed for the occasion, but it was no biggie. It was only Monday, and the judges said photographers would show up sometime that week.

But by the time I was heading to Algebra III, my last period class on *Tuesday*, I was a bit disappointed that Brent was a no-show. I'd have to come up with an extra cute look for yet another day. At this rate, the pile of reject clothes that I created that morning would only rise higher as the week went on. I didn't think I could keep this up for three more days.

Lost in thought, I wasn't focused on ignoring Rick as usual. Not even bothering to take the back way to my desk, I made a beeline from the front blackboard. Aside from the occasional Rick sighting at my volleyball games, algebra was the only time we were guaranteed to cross paths. In fact— as unluck would have it—my assigned seat was *right next to* Rick's. For weeks following our breakup, I had a crick in my neck from keeping my head rigidly straight. I barely even sneezed in his direction.

The class chatter quieted down as soon as our notoriously strict math teacher, Mr. Asante, entered the room. His back looked firm even though he was carrying a few hefty books. The man has become a legend at Teawood High and in the entire school district. Because he has zero tolerance, kids call him Mr. Z—but not to his face. It's not that he's intimidating in a menacing, loud way. Mr. Z doesn't raise his voice and he's not even a towering figure. His old-school teaching swag is influenced by his West African roots. He translates his traditional approach enough for us Westerners to understand. For example, he allows no excuses—especially because of all the luxuries and trimmings he says we get living a middle-class American lifestyle. Laziness is not tolerated. Blame no one but yourself for your failures. And so on. These are only his caveats. His actual rules are an entirely different animal.

Back in September, resentful kids tried but failed to blame their low grades on what they called an inability to understand Mr. Z's foreign accent. When enabler-type parents took the complaint to the principal, Z pointed to the neat, tidy numbers on the board and noted, "I don't *write* with an accent."

I took out my notebook and copied the

elegant equations he was now writing on the board. From the corner of my eye I could see Unslick Rick checking me out. Even though I was rocking a trendy H&M jumpsuit, I didn't get why he was staring. A month ago, when I was dressed up for an after-school event, he didn't take any notice. I wondered what all the fuss was today. Despite Mr. Z's keep-your-focus-on-your-own-desk policy, Rick's eyeballs were all up in my business. It's like guys have radar for when a girl has stopped thinking about them. *I think he can smell that my mind is on another guy* went my internal aha moment.

"Yo, London," whispered Rick, who was now slouching toward my desk. He leaned down and looked me in my eye for the first time in probably months. "Let me borrow a pencil?"

I could see that he already had a pencil on his desk. A dull, short one no longer than a preschooler's thumb, but a working pencil nonetheless.

It had become sort of a hater move. Kids in this class knew all too well that one of the rules was "Borrowing is permitted. Lending is prohibited." If you were caught lending someone anything, you—not the borrower—paid the price. Instead of penalizing the unprepared person, it pointed a finger at the lender's enabler tendencies.

If you got caught, Mr. Z didn't blow up your spot in front of everyone. He simply made a note of your offense in his grade book. Come report card time, you'd be the one scratching your head and wondering why your average was a few points lower than calculated.

So with this in mind, anyone who tried to make a lender out of another student was just doing it to mess with their GPA. It was the closest thing to "fun" kids could have in this class.

I ignored Rick (and the beating in my chest) outright. When he asked again—this time with a flirty look in his eye and a playfulness in his voice—I betrayed myself by looking at him. He saw this as a good sign and smiled. His eyes searched my face and then rolled down from my lips to my shoulders and then to my chest.

I didn't know what he was reminiscing about because we never took it *there*.

Time to shut it down. I'd already given away too much of my feelings. I pretended to look bored with Rick and then rolled my eyes and focused on the board. It seemed to work. Rick was back to his usual slouching-away-from-dumped-ex-girlfriend position in his seat.

"I know the tricks because I have *beeen* a stu-*dant* before," Mr. Z was saying to a kid fighting sleep in the most obvious way. "You have *nevah beeen* a *tee*-cha."

Apparently, Rick wasn't the only one who was trying to run game during this period.

When the bell rang, I dashed toward the exit. I thought rushing would give Unslick Rick the hint not to walk me to my locker or anything. But that was arrogant thinking. My final glimpse of him proved dude wasn't even checking for me. He was smoothing down his nonexistent goatee and staring *hard* at some girl's legs.

Such a user.

I didn't know why I felt bothered. This should've come as no surprise to me. I mean, it was obvious he was just messing with my head during class. The boy had no sense of remorse and no genuine feelings. If it were up to him, he'd have me humping his ankle like a puppy dog and begging for a tummy rub.

To think, Rick used to be a decent person. Unless I was totally blind to his shadiness, he was not the same guy I used to go out with. It amazed me how in just one summer, Rick's head grew at the same rate as his athletic skills. He was clearly one of those people who would deny his own mama if he ever made it big. I didn't even recognize him anymore. It was no use thinking about our relationship. Everything we'd talked about or done over the eight months we hung out together now felt like a lie.

Considering my poor judgment in choosing Rick as a boyfriend, I wondered if setting my sights on Brent was such a great idea. When I met Rick, I was just hanging with friends so I was totally being myself. The fact that I was supposed to try to live up to some model persona was way above my pay grade and out of my league. *Why did I have to fall for an aspiring fashion photographer?* After his zooming in on gorgeous girls' faces and *Lawd* knows what else, I wondered how someone like me would measure up.

I was looking forward to that afternoon's home v-ball game. Not only did I need to work off the frustration from these past two days but I could use a pick-me-up. Volleyball made me happy. And on the court, I could forget that I was still scrambling to get my money right.

If only I could play every day.

The echo of sneakers squeaking against the gym floor commingled with crowd chaos and tight fists pounding (and open palms smacking) volleyballs. These are the sounds that put me at ease. I get a bit nervous before every game, but it's healthy anxiety that fades minutes after the starting whistle. It usually takes a few contacts with the ball to get me in a good groove.

I stood at the net, waiting for that moment. The game had just started. My black uniform shorts and red and black top fit snug and my socks were pulled up to my knees. My muscles tensed in anticipation of my first contact with the ball. I watched as our star setter positioned the ball perfectly into my airspace. I jumped to meet it with my fist and sent it jetting over the net. No sooner had I hit it than it returned straight back to me like a bullet. I sprang up and stretched my arms over my head, but the shot pierced my barrier. Thankfully, Star

Setter was there with a save that kept the ball in play. When it finally smacked the other team's floor, the home crowd roared and the scoreboard tallied and flashed. I high-fived SS and knocked elbows with my other teammates.

By the last quarter, we were ahead two sets. I was in a groove until the flash of a camera caught my eye. After I'd blinked away the red dots from my vision, the person behind the flash came into focus. It was Brent.

I couldn't believe it. I was sweating like a hog. It was to the point that beads that had trailed from my brow down my hilly cheeks were dropping from my chin. And my *hurr* was a hot mess. Thank goodness I'd doubled up on hair bands, otherwise I would've been looking like I was hit by lightning or experiencing static shock. I could do nothing about my bleeding elbow and the sweat marks on my shirt. There's no way a camera could pull cuteness from this picture. After all my tactical outfit planning, it was just my luck that he chose to show up when I looked my worse.

He flashed two more times as the coach on the other team called time-out and my team huddled for one last strategy session. I rushed to the sidelines and chugged down some water. The towel hanging off my seat hadn't been used so I wiped my face and behind my neck as quickly as I could. I splashed some water in my hands and wiped the blood from my elbow. *That should do it,* I thought.

"Now go back in there and finish this up, ladies." Coach Pat's jaw was tight and her eyes piercing. She was like a gambler in Vegas and I was happy for her. The lady is addicted to winning.

"One, two, three—," our team captain shouted.

The rest of us stacked our hands on top of hers and shouted back "*Go* Lady Warriors!" before hitting the court.

As soon as our victory was handed down to us, we met the other team at the net and shook their hands. They were always fun to play against. It was like we split up wins with them by losing every other meeting. This game broke that streak, since we had now won our last two matchups. It was an exciting thing to happen. Home-court advantage is the truth.

My teammates and I congratulated one

another. It's great how well we play together. It took a while for me to be able to read them as well as I can now. And with each game, the vibe grows stronger. We have our bad days, but this was definitely not one of them.

"Go L-Boogie!" I heard Pam shout from the stands.

I put my hand up, gave her a number one sign, and smiled.

I saw no sign of Brent. I'd forgotten about the bad timing of his lens somewhere during the last ten minutes of the game as things got intense and I got back in the zone.

It was a good thing he was gone. I wouldn't have wanted to face him now. I was too excited about the win, and thinking about an out-of-my-league crush would've spoiled my buzz.

I showered and then threw on a pair of jeans and a fresh jersey. I slung my black gym bag over my shoulder and pushed my way through the heavy locker-room door to the hallway.

I came face-to-face with Brent. He was waiting in the hallway. For an airheaded second, I wondered who he was waiting for.

Does he know anyone else on my team? I wondered.

"Hey, London." He walked toward me, his hands in his pockets and his camera equipment on his shoulder. He looked cute. He was wearing another button-down shirt, but this time he'd left it open and paired it with a graffiti-scribbled T-shirt and jeans. His hair looked freshly touched-up, like he'd just come back from the barber shop. And his brown face was glowing as if he'd smoothed it down with some cocoa butter. He looked like he smelled good.

"Hey," I said, my voice trailing a bit. I cleared my throat and switched my bag to my left shoulder. I wanted to keep the sweaty scent wafting from the dirty uniform far away from him.

"Great game." I was glad he was in more of a talkative mood than I was. "I got some crazy shots of you." He sounded a bit more enthusiastic than someone talking to a gold medalist of the Sweat Olympics should be.

"As wild as I was looking out there?" I half-joked and half-fished for a compliment. "That can't be."

"I'm tellin' you." His energy surprised

me—and made me smile in spite of my nervousness. "If you don't have to be anywhere, can I show some of them to you?"

Now that caught me off guard.

"Uh, okay." I didn't want to let too long of a silence follow his question. "But we have to clear out of here pretty soon."

"Yeah, I heard the 'no loitering' announcement." The dimple on one side of his smooth face deepened when he smiled. "I was thinking maybe we can walk to a spot on the Ave?"

He was thinking *we* . . . ? How long had he been thinking *we*? I wanted to do the "chicken noodle soup and a soda on the side" dance. But he couldn't tell that by looking at me—until my eyebrows twitched one after the other like they were doing the wave at the Super Bowl.

"Cool." I'd had to say something nonchalant to cover up that display.

Apart from my "thank you's" the few times he held open the heavy doors, we walked in complete silence. It wasn't an uncomfortable silence, but rather a polite one, if such a silence exists. By the time we exited the front door of the school, there were only a few stragglers and cars left.

"Hey, London!" I heard Pam shout from across the street. She and her boyfriend Jake were about to get into his beat-up blue Corolla. "You wanna ride?"

Heaven bless her, but Pam had the worst timing sometimes. She meant well, but I wanted the extra time to be alone with Brent.

"Uh, nah, that's okay," I called out, turning away from Brent so only Pam could view the exaggerated "not now" expression on my face. "I'm not going home. Thanks, though."

"Where you headin'?" Pam kept digging. I'd forgotten who I was dealing with. Even if I had climbed a lamppost to shine a light on my expression, Pam wouldn't have been able to clearly see it. She's not nicknamed Batgirl for nothing.

There was no way to play this but to answer her questions. I took a few steps closer to the curb so I didn't have to put my business on blast.

"Just to the Ave." I made it sound like it was no big deal to walk the four residential blocks. Which it wasn't.

"It's getting dark," mama Pam answered. "I'll take you."

I looked at Brent, who seemed amused by the back-and-forth. Pam's boyfriend didn't add anything to the conversation. He doesn't disagree with her much. The jury's still out on whether that's out of fear or respect.

"Do you mind hopping in with me?" I asked Brent.

"Not a problem," he answered like a trouper. "Cool of her to offer."

When I got into the car, Pam continued in her mama mode.

"Hey, London," Jake greeted me as I stepped in the car.

"Wassup, Jake." I buckled in.

"Aren't you gonna introduce us to your friend?" Pam asked, her rearview mirror reflecting the mischievous grin on her face.

"Pam, Jake, this is Brent, a photographer with the contest."

"Oh!!" Pam, in true signature theatrics, bounced so high out of her seat, her head bumped the car ceiling. A piece of torn lining that had been discreetly tucked was knocked unraveled and now hung next to her head. She excitedly twisted around to face us.

My eyebrows were trying to send Pam

all sorts of messages in Morse code or with smoke signals or flashing lights (read: through my eyeballs) or anything else I could send off undetected. *Please resist that drama gene,* they were screaming. Brent shifted in his seat as if nervously preparing to be put on the spot. He was probably thinking of the safest way to roll out of a moving car.

And like a hooptie miracle, Pam rebuked the drama, but suddenly looked like a deer in headlights. "I don't wanna embarrass my gurl London," she began, on a desperate hunt to find the right words to play off the whole reaction. I took a few cautious breaths. "But it's just that I . . . uh . . . I adore Cynthea Bey."

Good save. I quietly exhaled.

"No, I can understand." Brent's jaw relaxed. "My sister feels the same way about her. I've got some candid shots of her posted up on Flickr. You should check it out."

"I will. I'll look up your page."

Pam wouldn't start up an embarrassing conversation from there. And she didn't. Not because of any lack of curiosity. Her silence had as much to do with her having my back as it did with the loud reggaeton thumping from the speakers. I caught her looking at me in the rearview three times in the short ride.

"Thanks," I told Pam when we got out the car; I meant it in more ways than one.

There was a smattering of people strolling the Ave. I suggested we go to Juiced! juice bar. It's a cute little spot I like to hit after a game. Forty-five minutes of intense volleyball usually makes me feel like I can down all the fruity fluids in the world.

"Thanks," I said as I walked through yet another door held open for me by babelicious Brent. But "No thank you" is what I swiftly replied when he offered to carry my shoulder bag of funk. The boy was a black belt in the art of being a gentleman. He flexed his gallant swag in subtle, unannoying ways. Like, thank goodness that when we climbed out of Jake's ride from both sides of the car, Brent didn't scurry over like Quasimodo to open my door and assist me out from my side.

Not willing to get too excited about his kind gestures, I reminded myself of the lesson learned from Pam's past crush story. The moral of that one was that a guy's thoughtful or polite acts do not necessarily signify he's wooing you. Offering his seat is not synonymous with offering his heart. Some of them actually do it because they want to, not because they want *you*.

The inside of Juiced! is set up like a fitness gym. The cashiers dress like personal trainers and wall sconces that resemble barbells hang next to wall mirrors, lockers, and a ballet barre.

"Wanna grab that table by the window?" Brent asked. "I'll go get the drinks. Let me guess—you're a Pineapple Delight kind of girl?"

He was offering to pay? I couldn't let him do that.

"No, I—"

"My bad," he said, cutting me off. "I didn't peg you for the açai and pomegranate type."

"That's not what I was saying no to." I chuckled.

"Aw, c'mon. I owe you at least two dollars—*remember?*" Brent smirked recalling my lame opening line. "And you're the star player of the night, so it's my treat."

"Medium mango smoothie." I gave in.

A few minutes later, Brent returned carrying my smoothie and what appeared to be a large Strawberry Protein Blast for himself. It's a shame that I can identify all the drinks in this place. This is the type of shop I'd feel more at home working in. Unfortunately, when I was job hunting, the Juiced! manager told me they had a hiring freeze.

Brent raised his drink and saluted me with it. "Here's to your digs, kills, and shanks."

"Wow, you make it sound like I'm skilled in prison yard activities." As I laughed, I hoped there was nothing stuck in my front teeth.

"Well, *some*body needs to call the guards on you—you're a beast on the court." He smiled and looked at me with his deep-set, dark eyes. I wondered whether Brent's sense of judgment was more Paula Abdul or Simon Cowell.

"Let me show you," he said.

Brent ruffled through his leather case and pressed a few buttons on his camera before leaning across the table to share his LCD screen.

It was a shot of me jumping up for a block at the net. I'd had no idea Brent was snapping at that moment. My hands were about to make contact with the ball, and my feet seemed so high off the ground, it was like I was levitating. I hadn't known I could do that. I was amazed.

"Wow," I told him. "That is nasty!"

He looked proud.

"And check these out." He started scrolling backward, looking for more action shots. There was another one of me in midair with the ball inches away from my open palm. In the next frame, I was spiking the ball with all my might. It was a relief to see that the sweat dripping off my face during the game was picked up as healthy, glistening skin on camera. Brent also got a shot of me nailing a dig. I was bent on one knee with my other leg outstretched to the side. My lips were pursed in determination, my arms were extended, and my hands were clasped in a tight fist.

"You sure these are for Face and not *Sports Illustrated*?" I asked Brent, impressed with his work. "These are dope! And I'm not just saying that because they're of me."

Brent nodded as he chuckled. "No, I really am as amazed as you are."

His honesty was surprising. Someone like Unslick Rick would never admit that they weren't 100 percent in control.

"Really? I took you for a photographer

heavy into his game." I had slipped too quickly. I didn't want to let on that I had noticed him so closely that day at Art Attack. "It's just that I don't know anyone my age with an internship at a big company." I said, trying to recover from my last comment.

"It was wild how I got that job," Brent started. "I work at a barber shop on the other side of the Ave. I've mostly been sweeping up hair off the floors there for about a year. But a few months ago, I started taking crazy-angle portraits of client hairstyles and my boss put them all over the shop. Turns out one of our regulars works in Face's production department. He liked the shots so much, he mentioned me to Didier."

"And the rest is history," I added with renewed fascination in this cutie.

Brent pressed buttons on his camera, resuming the presentation of game-time pics. There were a lot of them.

When I leaned over the table to get a closer look at his slideshow, we accidentally bumped heads.

"Oh, sorry." We apologized at the same time and chuckled sheepishly.

"You okay?" Brent sounded concerned,

like he was holding back the urge to rub my forehead for me.

"I'm fine." I smiled, lowering my eyes to the screen.

"Maybe I should sit next to you so you can see better," he offered.

I didn't protest.

By the time I scooted over, Brent was already out of his seat and next to me. I was glad my smelly gym bag was underneath the table and zipped all the way. But then again, the bag of funk could've proven a much-needed distraction. I was all types of nervous having him so near. Not knowing what to do with my hands, I held on to my cold drink glass. My grip around it tightened when Brent's shoulder softly grazed mine during the slideshow.

"You know," he continued, not seeming as affected by our intimate seating arrangement as I was. From this close, I could see the tiny black flecks in his dark brown eyes. "Ever since I found out about photographer Gordon Parks, I wanted to be just like him."

"Gordon Parks of the seventies blaxpoitation films?" I wanted to make sure we were on the same page.

Brent paused to smile at me. He looked impressed that I knew something about his hero.

"Yes, that's the one." He moved aside his drink to make room for his enthusiasm. Once he got going, this shy guy could talk.

"But Gordon Parks was a legend in more ways than old 'Shaft' movies. He was a photographer who shot famous portraits and fashion features. He was the first black photographer to work for *Vogue*."

"Wow." Now it was my turn to be impressed. It was so cute watching Brent talk about something with so much passion.

"The guy was phenomenal. I wanted to be just like Gordon and follow in his footsteps," he said. "That's why I'm interning at Face. Their portraits and fashion photography are cutting-edge."

"I have to admit that even though I'm not the creative type, I love their site," I agreed.

"Yeah, but hearing the crowds today, timing the shots just right, and anticipating the action on the court got me amped. I was pumped like never before. And now I'm looking at these shots I took like, 'Whoa.'"

"So, are you thinking maybe of switching gears?"

"Well, all I'm saying is I like how this felt and I want to do more of it. See where it takes me." He was being honest about his uncertainty. I could definitely relate to that.

"What about you?" He studied my face. "Plan on going pro? You were doing your thang out there. You're a natural."

My cheeks tingled and got warm.

"Well, it would be a dream to represent the U.S. at the Olympics, but I'm not sure I'm ready for the big time."

"Why not?" He said, challenging my doubt.

"Let's just say, my skill level is not worthy of shining that division's shoes. But my plan is to go to a summer camp where I can train with some of them."

"Oh, really?" He genuinely seemed interested. "When?"

"This summer. That's why I'm busting my butt working part-time. I need to raise the tuition so I can go."

"Well, I hope you do get that shot." Brent's voice got softer as he fumbled with his camera. I looked down to the screen and saw that he was zooming on my face in one of the photos.

I swallowed hard.

He continued, "Because you really look good out there."

I wasn't sure if he meant that in more ways than one. A hurried sip of my mango smoothie slowed down my quickened breath.

When I put down my drink and glanced up at him, he was staring intently at me.

Six

"How was the game, honey?" my mom called out from the kitchen when she heard me come through the front door. Dad was sunk deep into the chaise lounge as he watched the evening news—all six feet, four inches of him.

My parents usually try to make it to my games, but lately Warren and Wyatt's after-school schedule was hemming them up in car-pooling duties. The latest craze was shuttling Warren to spelling bee trials and Wyatt to Little League.

"It was great." I stopped shouting when she walked into the living room. My dad plucked himself out of the quicksand chair and sat up. The poor thing tried to look interested even though he was dead tired and half asleep. "We won!"

"Excellent." Dad got a second wind and held out his fist for me to dap. "That's what I'm talking 'bout. It's the old Abrams touch," he boasted.

"That's okay," Mom teased, doing her happy two-step dance past Dad. "Because she gets her smarts from the Vincent half of her genes. *Haaay!*"

After seventeen years of marriage, Mom still didn't think of herself as an Abrams. Who can blame her when my grandmother always acted so salty to Mom? The two just never got along, mostly because Grandma Abrams couldn't bring herself to respect a woman who let her husband outcook her.

Dad half-smirked and gave my mother a playful tap on some body part I didn't want to be a witness to. I turned away and headed to my room where it was safe.

"Wait," Mom called after me. I stopped at the first staircase step, resting my elbow on the banister. "Guess who I ran into today at the supermarket?"

I shrugged my shoulders.

"Mrs. Fletcher. Remember her? Kelly's mom?" I braced myself. "Why didn't you tell me Kelly's also taking part in this modeling contest?"

The strained smile on her face made me nervous.

"No particular reason," I answered, careful not to make any sudden moves. If I were to make it out of this conversation unscathed, the key would be to escape slowly and deliberately. "I didn't think it was a big deal."

"I'm not saying it *is* a big deal." Her nostrils flared, but her smile stayed tense. "But it's the type of information that I find interesting to know."

"Okay." I looked to my dad for help, but his eyes were half closed. "Well, I better get upstairs."

"Aren't you hungry?" Mom asked. It was Tuesday, which meant that Dad had cooked his slammin' salmon dish.

"I'll be down in a minute. I wanna make a quick phone call," I said over my shoulder.

That was awkward.

In my room, safe from my mother's Stage Mom alter ego, I fired up my laptop to see if Pam was online. She wasn't. I was thinking of a million things at the same time. *Would my volleyball photos be posted on Face's site that quickly?* That would feel totally weird. It was odd enough seeing my face on the contest home page. I clicked around the site, looking for updates.

"London, you said you'd quiz me on my words tonight." Warren nearly made me jump out of my skin. I hadn't even heard him come into the room.

"You can't just be rollin' up in here," I snapped. Wyatt was usually the bugaboo of the two, so I felt instantly guilty for going hard at the more sensitive twin.

"Just give me a half hour." I softened my tone. "I'll come get you."

After he left, I looked through the initial head shots of all fifteen contestants that were still featured on Facemag.com. *There I go*, I thought as I clicked on my photo.

It's weird—I didn't feel any more popular since the whole thing started. I'd been too busy with school, volleyball, and the contest. But I had noticed that the occasional classmate who'd never spoken to me before would stop me in the hallway to comment on my Web page or congratulate me about getting selected.

Overall, kids at Teawood High don't stress events like this. A few students had entertainment exec parents or relatives "in the industry." Plus, TV cameras have been in the school before, shooting commercials or reality-show episodes. It wasn't that huge a deal—or at least people pretended like it wasn't.

When I got Pam on the phone, she asked me how it felt to be a local celebrity.

"That word is heavy." I grimaced. "I can't even imagine what it must be like for true famous people. It was bad enough having a paparazzi-type experience with Brent today."

Mentioning Brent was a perfect segue into updating Pam about the after-game drinks. So as not to interrupt my story, she barely breathed while I recapped.

"Besides being a cutie who I want to take me in his arms and worship me," I told her, "he's cool people. We really just vibed."

When my mom knocked on the door, I dashed off the phone.

"Hey." She poked her head in. She always has a radar for when something is up. "I put the food aside for you. I'm heading out soon to pick up Wyatt."

"N'kay." I pretended to be hard at work on my laptop. Really, I had just refreshed the contest page. The icon with the flashing camera bulb signaled that new photos had just been posted.

"What's that about?" Mom was standing behind me, craning her neck to see what I was doing. "Ooh, click on it and let's see what's been updated!" she said, pulling up a chair beside me before I could protest.

I should've been more careful. Not for my own good, but for my mother's. I didn't want to feed her with false expectations. Once she gets excited about something, she puts her heart into it and sets herself up for disappointment. Especially when it comes to the girly dreams she has for me, her only daughter.

"What are you waiting for?" She nudged me on the shoulder to snap me into action.

"I thought you had to leave now to pick up Wyatt?" I stalled.

"I was leaving early just to eavesdrop—you know me." She looked like she'd damn near forgotten she had another child to bring home. "I'll leave in a few minutes."

When I refreshed the site, a few contestants' surprise-visit photos were already posted—but thankfully, not mine. I scrolled through two contenders' photos, avoiding one girl's in particular.

"Let's see what Kelly's photos look like." My mother was so predictable sometimes. I obliged.

Kelly's photos had my mom blinking more times than a bad liar. The surprise photographer had followed Kelly to after-school hang-out spots. She looked like a glam goddess sipping from a coffee mug at a sidewalk café. The photo's angle spotlighted her crossed legs, which were wrapped in black tights and dipped in leather knee-high boots. She looked a vision of Parisian style in her gray sweater dress.

Twenty comments were already posted. Readers were gushing over her "fab-u sense of style" and "model good looks."

I wanted to quickly click through but my mom was hooked. She was reading comments and studying the photos.

"That's okay, London, sweetie," she said despite the fact that I didn't need consoling. "You don't have to worry about that Ms. Fletcher. You've always been able to out-smart that *chile* anyway."

"Really, Mom, I'm okay," I assured her. If only she knew that Brent was my biggest concern in this competition. Not Kelly and what she thought of me.

"I've got it!" Mom totally ignored me and sprang out of her chair like she'd had an epiphany. I braced myself for what she was about to suggest. "Why don't you get Pam and her hotshot makeup artist cousin to give you some easy and quick tips!"

I was a bit offended. She wanted me to pretty myself up. That felt like a blow and a confirmation that Mom really did think of me as unattractive. But then I thought about my sorry attempt at sprucing up earlier that week when I was expecting Brent to surprise me. Although I realized that I could use some styling help, I didn't want to admit it to my mom, who should've been feeling mad guilty now for insulting me.

"Hey, hun, you're gonna be late." Dad popped his groggy head into my room to rush Mom.

"Here I come," she told him and then practically skipped out of the room. "Call Pam right now and get on it!" she squealed like a schoolgirl on prom night. Then she started speed talking: "*Thisisgonnabesoexciting.* But I won't crowd you. It's okay if I'm not invited to your makeover session. I like to be surprised by the big reveal anyway." Her last words trailed into the hallway over her shoulder.

Do I even have an opinion in the matter? I thought.

The photos from my volleyball game were posted on Face's site the next afternoon. By the time I got home from school, there were close to fifty comments on my page. Almost all of the comments (and I read them all) raved about the photos of me working it out on the volleyball court. "Kickass" wrote one and "Powergurls unite" posted another. But what especially got me was how much readers identified with me. One post read "Finally—a *real* girl is represented in a modeling contest."

Those two words were repeated over and over again in a lot of the posts: "real girl." The overwhelming support not only boosted my mood but it could advance me in the contest standing. Thanks to online reader votes, I had the potential to dodge another week of eliminations. (On Saturday the judges would be saying sayonara to another three contestants.)

It felt good to have support. If I got enough votes to stay in the game, I was ready to accept the fact that I really had a place in this competition. Regardless of how I'd gotten into this, it was getting more real-deal by the minute.

"Come on in, gurl." Pam greeted me in front of her cousin's apartment building. "And stop looking so nervous. This is gonna be fun!"

"You know I'm not crazy about makeup." I warned Pam not to expect me to stay agreeable through this experience. "The last time you tried to paint my face, I felt like a freakin' clown."

"My cousin Layla has been informed of all of your hang-ups," Pam said like an agent. "She promises to ignore your whining."

Despite my whining, I was grateful that they had agreed to hook me up. Pam's cousin had worked magic on some cool B-list singers—and a few A-listers before they made it big.

When the elevator doors opened on the third floor, Layla was there to meet us. I hadn't seen her in over two years. But again, it struck me how some cousins can look so much alike. Pam and Layla both have soft round faces, wide-set eyes, and the cutest button noses (minus any trace of a nose bridge). They're about the same medium height and both are blessed with the kind of supershapely body that causes guys they cross paths with to get whiplash. The only difference is, Layla's complexion is a few shades darker and she has shoulder-length locks. (Layla once schooled me about never calling them "*dread*locks.")

Today she was wearing her locks in a high ponytail pulled to one side of her face. Her huge hoop earrings matched the silver bangles on her wrist. She styled out a snug white T and jeans with a loosely knotted neon yellow tie and a tiny fitted cream vest.

"This way, please," Layla said, guiding me into her apartment and straight to the makeup chair. She had me facing away from the mirror that was framed with showgirl lights.

"Now let's get working on those thick eyebrows." Layla looked anxious to get started. I could sense that she enjoyed that I was a blank canvas. She started plucking and it didn't feel nearly as painful as I thought it would. My back, at first tense and stiff, began to melt into the chair's contours as I relaxed.

Next Layla removed my hair band and started to undo my ponytail. She had such a gentle touch, I didn't feel the usual tugs and yanks I endure when I get my hair straightened at the salon. Hoping that I was in for a head massage, I closed my eyes and started to drift a bit. Too bad that when she let my hair out in all its bushy glory, Layla decided to put off styling it until after makeup.

Pam excitedly showed me a few hairstyle photos she'd torn from magazines. One was of a model with hair as thick and curly as mine. One cornrow snaked from the left side of her face, over her forehead, and ended on the right side. It sort of looked like a crown.

"This would look so cute on you." She seemed as excited as my mom. I got the sinking feeling that everyone had been secretly hoping and praying that I would one day agree to a makeover.

"Or look at this girl's hair." Pam flapped another torn magazine photo in front of my face.

It was of a girl who wore her hair tightly pulled up to the center of her head with the ends left to hang over one side, like a funky, curly girl faux-hawk.

"I like it." I was surprised that I identified with the bold look. It was both sporty and stylish.

Layla wanted a closer peek at the hairstyle.

"This would work with the oval shape of your face," she said, offering her professional opinion. "And it would bring out those expressive eyebrows and high cheekbones of yours in a nice way."

"Well." I took a deep breath. "Let's go for it, then."

After forty-five minutes of girl talk and celebrity gossip, Layla asked me to turn to face the mirror for the first time. When I did, I almost didn't recognize myself.

I looked hot! My makeup was barely there, but it lent an extra glow to my brown skin. My eyebrows were neat and shapely, opening up my face a lot more. My hair was funky without being too showy.

"I love it," I told them and they cheered. Pam looked like a proud mother.

"I can actually handle this look," I said. "It's not too fabulous or too over the top." I wouldn't feel too weird walking through the school hallways like this. Outside of my teammates, no one would notice, because kids switched up their look all the time at my school. The only other person who might make a fuss would be Unslick Rick. But somehow I doubted that. He had gone back to ignoring my existence ever since that pencil borrowing attempt.

"I wouldn't have you walk outta here feeling like Paris instead of the London you are," Layla said. "Just think of it as a remix of your old self."

Pam clapped her hands and jumped up and down. I gave her a hug just to keep her feet on the ground and we laughed.

She grabbed her tiny camera and snapped a few shots of me.

"For my blog, of course." She winked. "Now let me hook up your gear."

Pam took my arm and pulled me over to Layla's crowded walk-in closet. "I brought some clothes over to show you."

A few minutes later I emerged from the bathroom wearing the outfit Pam had picked out for me. I felt fine wearing the tiny vest and long shirt with tights, but the tall heels had me tripping over myself.

After all, I'm the type of girl who spikes volleyballs, not wears spike heels.

"Those shoes are not gonna work." I was

glad Pam said it first. She got on her hands and knees and rummaged through the cluttered closet. "Here, try these." I took the wedge shoes she handed me. When I slid my feet into them, I felt like I was wearing elevated sneakers.

"Aaah." I sighed like an actor from those hemorrhoids-relief commercials. "That feels so much better."

Layla turned up the volume on her iPod dock.

"Now show us whatchya workin' wit!" she called out.

We all busted out our best moves to the thumping music.

Seven

A makeover has a way of making a girl feel refreshed. And it's amazing what it does for your confidence. Every time I walked past a mirror, I had to do a double take, like, *Is that me?* Thankfully, Layla showed me some easy hair and makeup skills that I was able to duplicate on my own.

On Saturday morning when I stood in Chic Boutique among the top twelve contestants, it felt good knowing that I was stepping up my game. There was a lot of activity going on—the center of the store looked like it was under construction. I didn't get a close enough look because once we walked in, we weren't allowed to venture more than a few feet into the boutique. Something was up.

Judging from his expression, I could tell Didier was surprised to see my upgraded style. He smiled, eyeing me from head to toe before he spoke.

"I want to start by saying *bravo* to you ladies for braving the shadow photographers this week. You all look striking in the photos," he said. "And a special congrats to Ms. Kelly Fletcher, who has been voted into the number one spot."

Kelly bent her knees as if winding up for a leap into the air, but her feet didn't leave solid ground. I wasn't surprised that she'd gotten the most votes. When I read some of her online comments, especially the one that referred to Kelly as "a poster child for the fly-girl lifestyle," I figured she had it in the bag.

"That was the good news," gloom-and-doom Asha began. "Now for the bad. It's time to announce the contestants who landed in the bottom three spots. When I say your names, please step forward."

Now comes the drawn-out suspense, I thought. But I was wrong. Asha immediately called out three girls and addressed them directly.

"On behalf of Cynthea Bey and Face, thank you for participating in our model search," she said sincerely. "We invite you back to attend the Face of Spring Gala that will cap off the final week of the contest."

With that the three girls, shoulders slumped, shook hands with each of the judges, and then quietly exited the boutique. *Wow, these folks are all about yanking off the Band-Aid quick-fast in a hurry.* There was no catchy send-off phrase like in all those reality shows on TV.

"The rest of you, please come this way," Asha instructed before leading the nine of us farther into the store.

A slightly raised platform extended from the counter out into the heart of the boutique shopping area. The long checkout counter was completely concealed behind makeshift curtains. The place was primed for a fashion show. But who would be putting it on?

I was too naive to think that *we* would be the models working that runway. Something in me clung to the idea that we were there to watch a demonstration of how a professional fashion show is run. But that didn't explain the mischievous smirks that were now on the judges' faces.

"In one hour, Chic Boutique will be

open for business as usual. But today, shoppers and a few invited guests will be the audience for your fashion show," Asha continued. I could tell she was excited because there was more than the usual dry tone in her voice.

"Our photographers will set up at different angles along this runway but you are not to look at the lens. Keep your focus on working the crowd and on showcasing the look you're wearing," Didier instructed. "We'll be examining your walk, your presentation, and finally, your photographic appeal."

I'd never ever been in a fashion show before. All I knew was there are enough YouTube clips of models taking stumbles on runways to keep me entertained for a lifetime. I wondered if this was karma cashing in, paying me back for laughing so hard at them—and for forwarding said clips to friends.

"The show will last thirty minutes, in which time you will each make *three* wardrobe changes. We know that sounds tight, but it's the perfect exercise to determine how efficient and professional you can be under pressure," Asha said, cutting into my thoughts.

They are setting us up for failure, I concluded. This was merely a way to find out who looked most graceful as they were screwing up.

"As always, today's photos will be posted on the site. But this time, video highlights and low points of the show will also be posted. You'll be able to read the comments we'll be collecting from our invited guests and from the shoppers."

I gulped when I imagined being the star of the "low points" clip.

"Behind that curtain is a clothing rack with your name on it, on which five outfits are hanging. You each will be assigned an assistant who will facilitate the changing process. Your hair and makeup will be done once, before the start of the show," explained Monica. "When I call your name, please make your way to the marked corner to get dolled up. The rest of you can go backstage to set up your dressing areas."

I was with the group who got the first look behind the curtains. We all had to share the area behind the L-shaped counter. I immediately moved my rack against the makeshift wall, using the barrier as a semi-private changing room.

"London, you're next with hair and makeup," Asha called out. She then rushed me over to the seat and mirror a few short yards away. No sooner had I sat down than fingertips were dotting my face with liquid foundation. I felt like I was on a beauty conveyor belt.

In the next hot minute, she was shooing me away. I looked at her quizzically. "What about—?"

"Your hair works as is," she said, reading my mind. I left with a smile on my face in spite of the growing knot in my stomach and the feverish pace this challenge was taking on.

Even though I wasn't gone long, most of the girls were already dressed by the time I got back to the changing area. I dashed behind my semiprivate area and started tearing off my clothes. My assistant reached over the rack to hand me a pair of rocker leather pants. Next was the top, which I zipped halfway up my back. Before heading to my assistant to zip up the rest, I paused to squeeze my feet into the heels that went with the outfit.

I could tell that the Chic Boutique doors had opened for business. The buzz of curious shoppers jump-started my nerves. I worked through the queasiness in my belly.

Pandemonium began almost right away. "Where's the other shoe?" one super-stressed-out contestant demanded of her assistant. The woman assisting me needed no prompting—not that I would ever use such a tone with a complete stranger. She kept up a fast pace.

Tribal rhythms broke from the speakers in one startling moment.

"Go, London, go!" Monica yanked my arm and fed me to the dogs waiting outside. My first nervous step on the runway was a wobbly one. The tall, slim heel felt weighty, which I hadn't expected. The move caused the rest of my leg and hip to jolt to one side, and I rushed to have my other leg steady myself. Both strides added up to a spring in my walk that caused my hair to bounce. I kept the pace to play it off and it turned out to be the perfect accident. The faces in the crowd were in approval of my sassy strut. I kept it up to the end of the runway.

When I rounded the platform and headed back, the excited buzz of the crowd fizzled. I'd forgotten about my half-zipped back. The lightweight rayon collar was already droopy, but my bouncy stroll had caused it to flop and open like a wilting flower. There was nothing I could do to stop the zipper from trailing down lower. I couldn't get behind the curtain fast enough.

Kelly entered the catwalk just as I stepped off. Everything she was wearing was fully zipped, buttoned or clasped. Fully. While everyone else was scrambling, she had barely broken a sweat. The girl was born for this stuff.

I could've sworn I heard the crowd "ooooh" and "ahhhh" while she was out there. They'd already forgotten about me.

On my way back to my changing rack, I took off my shoes. I immediately regretted doing that when I tripped over a belt strewn on the cramped floor. Just as I regained my footing, I stepped on an earring. It was like the changing area was set up with booby traps.

After I cleared the landmine of accessories, I reached my small area and started yanking off the skintight pants. They got stuck over my hips for a few seconds. When I finally freed myself of the last pant leg, Kelly was returning from the catwalk. Her rack was positioned a few feet away, perpendicular to mine. As much as I tried to concentrate on getting dressed, I couldn't help tuning into Kelly's corner of the makeshift changing room. *How is it that she gets ready so quickly and efficiently?* I wondered.

My competitive spirit kicked into high gear. Whether or not she realized it, I was the defense to her offense. She made a move—for instance, opting to put on her dress before her shoes—and I made a countermove to prove to myself that my way was working out faster. There was no way I would have her steal my thunder by wooing the crowd after I'd swayed them my way.

In a major way, Kelly helped me step up my game during the fashion show. Just like when I'm on the court; playing against a more skilled v-ball team is the best way to improve as a player. It also made the match-up so much more exciting.

Kelly noticed the quicker pace of my changing. She eyed me as I headed onstage with my gear game-tight. Not to be out-done, she threw on her final piece—an extra-long beaded necklace—and strutted my way, getting in line behind me.

My second trip to the stage was as seam-less as the dress I modeled. The audience's response was even more positive than my first time down the aisle. What's more, I couldn't tell the difference in the reaction Kelly got.

By the time I rounded the platform for the third time—thankfully, in flats this time—I flashed the crowd a smile of gratitude for being so supportive.

I caught up to Brent right outside Chic Boutique after the show. Since my Saturday shift was awarded to another coworker, I had the afternoon off. My only challenge was to let Brent know that I was free to hang without seeming like a groupie.

"Hey, Brent." I took a chance to brave the first move. He had just gotten off a call on his cell.

"Hey, yourself." Brent looked up and let a slow smile stretch his lips. "Good job out there today."

"It was brutal at first—but thank you," I answered, feeling giddy once again. "I don't know how many more of those surprise challenges my stomach can take."

"You'll be fine," he encouraged. "Just gotta keep your eyes on the prize, and things will slide off your back."

If only he knew I didn't prize a modeling

contract at all. We kept up a slow pace.

"Got a busy day ahead?" I asked. It felt awkward, but I had to make some kind of move toward hanging out together again. I didn't want to leave things to chance.

"No plans, really," he answered, unaware of where I was going with this. That meant I had to give him another hint.

"I'm headed to the bookstore. You're welcome to come along, if you want to." *There, I said it.*

Brent's dimple deepened. He seemed flattered.

"I want," he said simply. That made us both chuckle bashfully. For the short silence that followed, we both kept our eyes on the swirling leaves on the sidewalk as we slowly strolled. I couldn't believe I just asked a guy out. Well, sort of.

"Your friend Pam's been checking out my Flickr shots of Cynthea Bey," Brent said, leading the conversation.

"Yeah, she told me." I was glad the awkwardness had past. "She really likes your images."

"I haven't even posted the best ones yet. I haven't had time to update the stuff on there in a while."

"I know what you mean." I started to complain about my lack of time-management skills when something caught my attention. A delivery man carting boxes stacked up on a dolly barreled onto the sidewalk toward Brent. "Watch out," I warned.

I reached out and touched Brent's arm to alert him. He was wearing a sleeveless bubble vest, and I could feel his muscles through his long-sleeved polo shirt. I had no idea his arm would be so firm. Without realizing it, I let my hand linger before I finally moved it.

Brent narrowly escaped impact by stepping closer to my side of the sidewalk.

"I'm never gonna break even with you, huh?" he teased, the sun sparkling in his smiling eyes. "*Now* I owe you for saving my life."

We were still laughing when we walked into the bookstore a minute later.

The two-seater reading nook by the window was the perfect spot for us to chill. We stacked a few book and magazine selections on our shared table.

"So, any luck getting sports photography assignments?"

"Actually, yeah," he said. "I've been

talking with my school paper's sports editor about covering some games."

"That's great." I so admired how proactive he was being about this new goal.

"And you? Got your ticket to that summer camp yet?"

"I'm still coming up short in the cash department," I admitted. "It's about figuring out the best way to earn the money."

"Well, if you make an impact on the modeling contest, you'll be in the running for the cash prize," Brent said as if it were common knowledge.

"*Really?* There's a *cash prize?*" I leaned closer to him, my eyebrows raised.

"Aw, *man*," Brent grunted. "I didn't realize that was privileged info." He suddenly looked troubled. "Let me rewind—can we pretend I didn't say that?"

If it hadn't been for the knock on the storefront window, I might've stayed in shock from the news. From the sidewalk, Kelly was excitedly waving at us like we were all best friends. To make matters even more faketastic, she rushed inside to say hello.

"Um, please don't mention anything about the cash prize." Brent looked mad at himself for spilling the beans.

"No! I won't tell her anything about this," I assured Brent.

"Tell me anything about what?" Kelly was already on the scene and practically trembling with wide-eyed curiosity. She extended a hand to Brent. "Hey, I'm Kelly."

Brent shifted uncomfortably in his seat and forced out a smile.

"Tell me anything about *what*?" Kelly repeated with eagerness.

"Nothing." I downplayed the whole thing. "What's up?" I asked, as code for *What do you want?*

"I was just popping in to introduce myself to our contest photographer," She scanned both our faces for any clues. "But what's with this hush-here-she-comes vibe here? You guys keeping secrets?"

"Brent, Kelly and I go back to childhood, and for as long as I've known her, she's always been so . . . inquisitive," I said, even though I meant "nosy."

"Information is one of life's best tour guides." She smiled with contempt.

"Except when one is trespassing onto private property," I singsonged back.

Brent's eyes ping-ponged from me to Kelly and back again. It didn't look like he was over his slipup, and this back-and-forth wasn't helping him feel any better.

"Oh." Kelly sounded as if she had just been poked with a straight pin. "I'm sorry—am I disturbing you guys? I didn't realize we were allowed to hang out with the camera crew."

That did it. Kelly's observation seemed to push Brent's guilty conscious into action.

"It's okay—I'm heading out anyway." He got up in a hurry. I wanted to leave with him. "I'll catch y'all later."

"See you around," I called out after Brent, feeling sabotaged by Kelly.

Suddenly, Kelly looked deeply satisfied. She smirked down at me and walked off in the opposite direction, leaving me all alone in a nook for two.

Eight

I was going to have to miss yet another Saturday at work to attend the week-three meeting for the contest. My boss was cool about the first Saturday I missed. He thought the modeling contest was an unexpected and funny reason. But he might not be laughing this time.

Good thing my willingness to cover for everyone else had put me in a better position to ask for time off. But regardless of what the boss thought, my Saturdays were the quickest way for me to earn the money I needed for volleyball camp. I had to work two weekdays to equal the hours I got on just one Saturday. Because of my county's code laws, the shop (and most others) weren't open on Sundays.

While the idea of a contest cash prize was superexciting (not to mention, enticing), I couldn't let that throw me off my solo fund-raising efforts. I chose to stick it out in this competition way before I even knew about the money. I wasn't going to start letting it affect my decisions now.

Despite the pros and cons of missing a Saturday, come that morning, I reported to Teawood's performing arts center instead of Art Attack. My boss scheduled me for that afternoon so that I didn't have to miss the whole day. Unfortunately, that meant I wouldn't be putting in as many hours as I could've had I started in the morning. But it was better than nothing.

I wished my parents weren't always so firm. Would it kill them to fund my summer camp a year early? Would it kill them to change their minds?

"We'd lose credibility with you kids," my dad liked to explain. "And you all would think our words mean nothing."

Somehow, it never felt they were doing this for us.

The theater looked much larger with its empty rows of seats. I'd been there with my family months earlier to catch the summerstage August Wilson play. It had seemed a lot stuffier and tighter then.

"Welcome," I heard Monica, the judge from Cynthea Bey's modeling agency, say from the stage. "Please take a seat in the front rows and we'll get started in a few minutes."

I made my way to the front and scanned the seats for a spot. "Hi." I offered a friendly greeting to the contestant who made eye contact with me. But she blatantly didn't respond. At least not verbally—the shady side glance she threw at me was clearly another form of communication.

I thought I was early, but it looked like most of the girls had arrived. Everyone deliberately left an empty chair or two between themselves and the next girl. Although it was Week Three and there were nine contestants left, I had to sit in the third row just to keep up with the spacing. I made the effort to sit closer, but the girl I was going near shot me a fake smile right before dropping her bag in the chair two seats away from her.

I couldn't get used to how uncomfortable this felt for me. The tension sucked. Opponents on the volleyball court are way friendlier to one another. The girls in this contest would straight-up diss you when they were ready. Plus I felt like a big imposter among these stylish, pretty girls.

It's not that I expected this to be a sisterhood. Each girl was absorbed in her own world. And then there was the fact that we were all competing against one another . . .

A clang sounding from the stage grabbed my attention. A photographer's camera stand had tipped over and one of the other assistants was setting it upright again. Behind that assistant was Brent, unraveling an orange extension cord for the large lighting equipment.

It was nice to see him. He looked so professional up there among all that equipment. I kept watching as he unloaded more gadgets and plugged and unplugged wires from every direction.

How such a simple act could be so mesmerizing is beyond me. There wasn't anything else to watch. The other girls were either touching up their makeup in compact mirrors, texting people on their cell phones, or zoning out on their iPods. I was interested in the stage setup, and not just because of Brent. I've always been crazy about the stage—as an audience member and not an actual entertainer. My family caught a production or two every year. For me theater is as gripping as a juicy book or a sci-fi movie.

"So, congratulations on your jump in online popularity." Kelly's voice sounded so distant. As usual, the action onstage had pulled my attention away from reality. She had to repeat herself to get me to snap me out of it.

Kelly was fashionably almost late again and she'd slipped into the chair next to my bag without me realizing.

"Oh . . . thanks." I blinked until her face came into focus. She looked red-carpet and wind-machine ready, as always.

Had she seen me staring at Brent?

As if hearing my thoughts, Kelly's eyes searched the stage for the object of my fascination. Like a cat using its sixth sense, her eyes lingered on Brent before looking back at me. I could tell she wasn't going to leave well enough alone.

"Don't they have a great photo team?" she asked innocently. The question was bait. She was fishing.

"Yeah," I replied as nonchalantly as possible. Keeping my answers short was my only protection.

"Psst" came the soft whisper from the stage at that moment. I didn't think Brent would be hissing for my attention—nor would I respond to any guy who called me like that. But still, the unexpected sound sent my eyes up to Brent like a reflex.

Kelly's expression showed that she had caught the big kahuna. She smirked to herself as she glanced from Brent's face to mine. I pretended to be equally interested in the whole crew.

"Sorry about the other day in the bookstore," Kelly offered with a smidge of genuine warmth. "I didn't mean to intrude."

"No worries," I told her, unsure whether she was setting me up for something. Kelly and I had always managed to stay cordial with each other—no matter how crazy our parents would get. Now that we were older and competing again, I was sure her mother wasn't acting nearly as crazy as mine. But it was understandable that *my* mother was freaking. Kelly and her mother were probably chillin' because they couldn't possibly feel threatened by me.

"This is turning out to be a fun contest," she said.

"I know." I turned to face her. "And I'm

surprised I even made it this far." The minute I said it, I regretted setting myself up for her response.

"I'm surprised you made it this far too." She smiled as if she had just told me something sweet.

I could hear the TV announcer in my head now: *This gotcha moment was brought to you by the gullible heart of London Abrams. (Batteries sold separately.)*

The three judges walked onstage with grande-size drinks in hand. I noticed them right away, but for the iPod-plugged contestants, Didier put down his drink and clapped a few times. The acoustics carried the sound to our seats and everyone sat up.

"Ladies! Ladies!" he bellowed in perfect stage-actor pitch. "Thank you for joining us. Congratulations on making it through to the third week." His grin showed gusto for the progressing contest.

"You should all be proud of yourselves," Asha chimed in with a quarter of Didier's enthusiasm. "Your true personalities showed through in the photos that are receiving so much attention online right now. But today we're asking you to try something different." She walked around and dished out lots of eye contact for extra impact. "We're not meeting in a theater for the great elbow room," she continued. "We're here because today you will step into a character of the stage. We've collected an impressive line of famous costume designs from theater's most famous musicals."

I sat up and took short breaths. This was sounding more and more exciting by the minute.

Just then Didier rolled in a rack lined with garment bags on hangers.

"*Here*"—he paused for effect before continuing—"are your mystery costumes." Like a harp player grazing the strings, Didier ran his hand across the neatly arranged row of white garment bags. "Today your photo shoot is all about stepping into character. In case you're not familiar with the characters behind these fabulous costumes, there is a short written breakdown of each person we want you to bring out during your photo shoot."

Monica stepped forward carrying a clipboard. "Remember, as the Chic Boutique model, you're going to have to portray an image and assume different personas for the summer campaign. Here's your chance to show us you have that range. So when I call your name, please step up to collect your costume," she announced. "After all of your names have been called, follow me to the backstage dressing rooms."

"Maria of *West Side Story*" read the folded paper inside my designated garment bag. I didn't even have to read the character description. I was already very familiar with Maria and the musical. I heart *West Side Story*. It was one of my favorites in junior high. After seeing the movie and the musical, I couldn't get the songs "America," "Tonight," and "I Feel Pretty" out of my head.

The costume was a 1950s-inspired violet-colored dress. It was a button-down number with pretty short sleeves and a slender red pleather belt.

I slipped into the dress as quickly as possible. The judges hadn't announced who would be photographed first, but I didn't want to be the one who delayed the process. A pair of black peekaboo-toe heels were also in the wardrobe bag. Just as I slipped them on, Monica entered the dressing room and asked me and Maya (dressed as Elle Woods from *Legally Blonde: The Musical*) to follow her to another prep room.

It seemed like just yesterday I was sitting in the hair and makeup chair. Now here I was again sitting in front of an artist with a paintbrush in hand and my face was the canvas. The fun twist was that we would all be given wigs to match the era of our characters. The stylist lowered a short brunette wig over my head. The ends of the hair curled upward in a flip, which was also totally reminiscent of the 1950s. For a finishing touch, a wide, bright red plastic headband was pinched onto my head, holding the wig in place and adding extra pizzazz to my look. Next, the makeup artist painted on a thick, glossy layer of red lipstick. It's not the easiest thing matching red to dark brown skin. I watched as deeper purple tones were mixed into the red, creating a complementary plum red tint. For dramatic effect, the stylist glued fake eyelashes to my lids and painted on a character mole above my lips. I looked ready for center stage.

Monica inspected my look before she released me to the photo shoot. Before I was given the green light, she gave me a few chunky bracelets to wear on my left wrist.

"Looking good," she said approvingly. "Go see Didier."

My play BFF's eyes popped out of his head when he saw me approaching, my fluffy skirt swaying as I hurriedly reported to him.

"*Magnifique, Londres!*" he called out with a hint of vibrato in his voice.

I smiled in my usual shy way.

"Nuh-uh-uh." He waved his finger in the air. "You are not a shy contestant in a New Jersey modeling contest right now. For the next ten minutes, you are Maria of *West Side Story*."

And for the next ten minutes, I became Maria. I'd always admired her strength and sensibilities. As Didier cued up the songs from the musical's soundtrack, I started to draw on my memories of the character and began to relax. The head photographer seized the opportunity and began clicking away while he was pacing in front of me. Brent shadowed his movements, handing him different cameras every time he'd blindly reach back, holding out his hand like a doctor in the operating room.

It felt great being up onstage and pretending to be Maria. The self-conscious feelings creeping up didn't take hold. I shook them off and let the musical numbers transport me. I even mouthed along to the lyrics when "I Feel Pretty" came on. The photographer seemed to be running through all his film. Brent disappeared backstage with two of the used cameras and didn't resurface for the rest of my shoot.

"That was great," the lead photographer told me after his face emerged from behind the camera. "Thank you, Maria."

I curtseyed and walked offstage in the direction I came from. On my way there, I criss-crossed Maya, who was next to be photographed.

It was nice not to have a crowd of contestants watching my shoot. In this instance, it paid to go first. As I headed toward the stage-left exit, I heard the photo intern cue the *Legally Blonde* number "Bend and Snap." It made me smile and send a little wish for Maya to rock it out.

By the time I cornered the curtains and started down the backstage maze, I heard murmurings coming from behind a tall speaker. Kelly was talking in hushed tones. As I got a bit closer, I could see her red slip-on heels and second-skin black leather pants. I couldn't yet make out the rest of her because she was leaning over a table and out of my view. Two slow and quiet paces later, her black off-the-shoulder top and the back of the superteased blond wig she was wearing came into view. I braced myself to find out who it was she was whispering sweet nothings to at such close proximity and in such a quiet, dark, isolated area backstage. The person hadn't said anything back to her yet, but I had a good feeling who it might be.

I stomped a little harder as I walked. I wanted her to hear that someone was coming. But it was naive of me to hope that the presence of another person could make Kelly self-conscious. If I remember correctly, the girl flourishes when there is an audience. The sound of my deliberate footsteps caught her attention and she turned and stood upright for half a second. When she realized that it was me headed her way, she resumed her hushed conversation and—I swear I didn't imagine this—leaned in even closer. The view from where I was showed her rear end saluting the ceiling. *Lawd* only knew what view she was giving her companion.

The table Kelly was leaning on was now in full view. There was a scattering of film and camera parts on it. And as I finally reached Kelly, I was able to see Brent standing across from her.

Nine

Brent looked up from what he was writing on a spreadsheet when I came into his view.

There was no way to misinterpret the scene. Kelly was totally macking on Brent and giving it her all. The close lean-in, the hushed, soft voice, the seductive hint of boobage. And even I had to admit she looked damn amazing dressed as the sexy Sandy from *Grease*.

All of a sudden, I wasn't feeling "so pretty" as Maria anymore. Let's be real—the kind of stuff Maria wore was what Sandy wore *before* she got her sexy back. My look was feeling more matronly by the minute.

I paused when I saw Brent because I

was surprised. I knew that halting would translate into shock and disappointment. I didn't want to confirm Kelly's obvious suspicions about my crushing on one of the photo interns. And I didn't want Brent to think that he had some hold over me like that. So I played off my standstill and pretend to be lost.

"Oh no," I said. "I don't remember this being here. I must've made a wrong turn."

Brent, who had been paying extra-close attention to what he was logging on the spreadsheet and seemingly ignoring Kelly's advances, set down the equipment when I said this.

I think I caught a slight smile on his face as he looked at me.

If I didn't leave right then, I was afraid I wouldn't be able to hide my agitation much longer. Until recently, Kelly probably saw no difference between him and the lighting equipment. And now all of a sudden—and incidentally, after she noticed the attention I was bestowing on him—she wanted to flash him a bit of skin and whisper in his ear? It was too much of a coincidence.

Surprisingly though, Brent seemed unaffected by her feminine prowess or beauty.

"That's *aight*," he said. "Happens all the time."

He stuffed the final pieces in a leather case, zipped it, and slung it on his broad shoulder. "I'll show you how to get there," he said, walking away from the table and toward me.

I couldn't believe my SOS comment came out like a damsel-in-distress signal that he totally answered to. And Kelly couldn't believe it either. For a few seconds, it was like Brent and I forgot we weren't the only two people on the scene. Kelly made sure to remind us. She stood upright to face me and tapped one pedicured foot in annoyance.

"Wow, London, your sense of direction is about as bad as your timing."

Suddenly, Kelly didn't look so flawlessly gorgeous anymore. The ill things she was thinking about me had her face twisted up like a wicked witch's. It was clear that she didn't take too kindly to being upstaged. Especially when her original plan, which obviously backfired, was to stay solidly on the radar of every contest judge and crew member. Kelly had no doubt been blindsided by my relatively popular three-week run and my strong performance that day.

Normally, I would back away from the kind of challenge Kelly's actions were inviting. I'm the first person to acknowledge when I'm out of my league. I prefer to stick to my strengths. You won't catch me on *American Idol*'s delusional-rejects reels disagreeing with Simon's professional opinion. Besides, it is a known fact that if you don't care enough about what you are fighting for, you are less likely to win that battle. And if you had asked me a few weeks ago, I'd have confessed that I couldn't care less about modeling or winning this contest. The most I was looking to get out of this was more cozy encounters with Brent. As for everything else, I was just going with the flow and having fun.

But the Chic Boutique Model Search had become both an unexpected and welcome distraction for me. For the first time in months, I wasn't ping-ponging from the classroom to the court like the volleyballs that bullet over the net at my games. And the best part was all the awesome reader support I was getting for venturing out of my comfort zone. There were girls out there who got passed up and straight-up snubbed for not looking the part. I was representing them, a realization that stripped me of any tolerance for Kelly's sense of entitlement.

"I'm so sorry—I didn't realize I was interrupting anything," I offered with faux innocence.

"No, I was just finishing up here," Brent replied before Kelly could. Judging from his casual response, I could tell he didn't even take into account his alone time with Kelly.

"Kelly Fletcher, please report to the stage." Either that judge Monica walked on pointe or she was one of those weightless elves from *The Lord of the Rings*, because none of us heard her step onto the scene. We had no idea how long she'd been standing there. It caught us completely off guard and embarrassed the heck out of me.

Possibly from witnessing the tense exchange between Kelly and me, Monica raised an eyebrow disapprovingly before walking away.

"Guess you better get going." I nudged Kelly so she'd hit the road.

Kelly let out a heavy breath and shot me a look that vowed payback as she clip-clopped away.

"So, how did you enjoy the shoot?" I

loved the way Brent continued the conversation as if nothing off the hook had just happened.

"Great." I smiled despite feeling oddly worried.

"Good," he said, walking slower than necessary. I slowed my own pace down to stay in step with him. There were a few seconds of silent anticipation.

I was relieved when he spoke up first.

"Hey," he started, "I showed your volleyball photos to the editor at my school paper and she asked me to take some shots of tonight's boys' volleyball game at my school."

"That's really great!" We stopped walking to face each other. I was happy for him.

"Yeah, and I was thinking, do you want to meet me at the game?" he asked. "I mean— it's probably better if you bring a friend or two to hang out with since I'll be courtside taking pictures most of the time. But I was hoping maybe we could head to that juice bar afterward and talk some more."

If it looks and quacks like a duck, well then, duckie, it's a date. And Brent was asking me out on a date with him. Totally unexpected.

"Sure." I smiled, but not too deeply. "That sounds cool."

Before this moment, I was sure Brent would be totally turned off by me. Heaven knows he'd witnessed enough freestyle Kelly vs. London sparring matches to send him running far from me. It's embarrassing how easily we push each other's buttons. But now I was more inclined to believe Brent was actually interested in me.

"There he is." I pointed across the noisy gym at the guy in the brown cord jacket and jeans. Pam squinted in that direction, clearly not seeing anything. Her boyfriend Jake shook his head at her poor eyesight.

"Yeah—picture you pointing something out to Pam that's farther than three feet away." He chuckled.

"Never mind," I told them. "He's on his way over here."

Brent met us where we stood, between the water fountain and the gym's side double doors.

"Hey, London." He greeted me with a smile. His hair looked freshly touched up. His hairline was tight and his low fade seemed to glisten a bit. The perks of working at a barber shop.

"Hi," I answered, not sure if I should

give him a hug. To be safe, I did nothing but hang on to my bag with both hands.

I turned to my ace gurl to relieve the awkwardness I was feeling.

"Hey, Brent." Pam waved while Jake and Brent exchanged head-nods.

"Thanks for coming, guys." He seemed grateful that we came. "I'm not a part of my school's sports program but Warwick High has a reputation for winning so I'm excited to be shooting this game," he said, pretending to act like a museum tour guide.

"London knows all about this school's girls team's reputation for winning—right, gurl?" Pam joked.

"We only lost to them once this year," I said, defending the Teawood Warriors.

"Butchya only played 'em once." Pam wouldn't leave it alone.

"Ouch!" Jake exaggerated. He likes to make Pam feel good about anything she does—including telling corny jokes.

"Please," Brent cut through the oohs and aahs. "That's just because London sat out the last game against them. If she were playing, it would've been a different story."

Brent held out his fist and I bumped it with mine. He was defending me. This was definitely feeling like a double date.

"Let's go find a spot to sit before this place gets too crowded," Jake said.

"We'll meet you there," Pam said and we all wondered why. "I wanna get a quick drink of water. Wait with me, London?"

When the guys were out of earshot, Pam said, "You guys are so cute. And more importantly, I think he likes you!"

"Really?" I trust Pam's judgment of character.

"Yup, and—" Pam stopped short. Something caught her attention. "Don't look, but we have a stalker coming this way."

I took a peek anyway and saw Unslick Rick slithering his way toward us. Figures he'd be here. His star v-baller girlfriend was the captain of this school's girls team.

"How long has he been there?" I asked Pam.

"I don't know but he was staring hard at you with Brent."

Pam ducked down to grab a drink of water just as Rick came over.

"Hey, London." All of a sudden he was talking to me like we were cool. The tone of his voice was casual and friendly, like we'd just chatted yesterday.

I didn't respond right away. It still hurt every time I saw him. I wasn't over the humiliation and couldn't bring myself to be friends *or* be enemies with him.

"Hi," I finally answered dryly.

"I see you're here on a date?" he asked.

Pam apparently thought that was enough catch-up. She stopped drinking, wiped her mouth, and hooked her arm around mine.

"Let's get going, London," she said without any regard to him standing there. "The guys probably miss us by now."

We walked off without saying good-bye.

When we joined Brent and Jake in the upper bleachers, they were already deep in conversation. Jake was telling Brent about his favorite websites when Pam and I arrived on the scene.

"If anyone wants to book Jake's design services," Pam started, "they'll have to consult me first."

We continued vibing like this until a few minutes into the game, when Brent slipped away to start his photography work. The match was a fast-paced one. We cheered for the home team and they didn't disappoint. They laid down a thrashing on their visitors. It was almost painful.

At the end of the game I searched the court for Brent. He was at the net capturing an interesting angle on the traditional handshakes between the teams.

"We're gonna be late if we don't get going." Jake checked the time on the scoreboard.

"That's right." Pam turned to me. She'd told me that they had plans to catch the seven p.m. movie at the mall. They squeezed in this game because of me.

"Go 'head, guys," I told them. "Thanks so much for coming. I owe y'all one."

They didn't budge.

"I'll be fiiine," I said. "Now get outta here."

Pam wrapped her arms around me in a tight hug. Jake stood up and dusted off his fitted jeans and threw on his hoodie jacket with the huge skull graphic on the back.

I watched them walk out hand in hand and then turned my attention back to the right end of the court, where Brent was working.

"Hey," I heard Rick say from my left. "Somebody sitting here?"

What does he want? I wondered. I hadn't seen him during the game. Besides, I thought by this time he'd be canoodling in the bleachers with his star girlfriend.

That thought had me scanning the court for her tall, slender frame. I spotted her chatting with a sweaty player.

Rick took my silence as his green light to snuggle up next to me, typical opportunist that he is. I scooted over a few inches for fear of being seen sitting too closely to him.

"London," he started in a voice flooded with sensitivity. Anyone who didn't know better would shed a sentimental tear at the sound of it. "It's good to see you."

I looked at him and blinked a few times. *Am I imagining this?* His face looked solemn and his eyes searched mine. He licked his lips before pouring out a few more syrupy words.

"I know I don't deserve to even be talking to you after the way I treated you," he continued. This was the first time he was even mentioning, much less acknowledging, the Incident. Just talking about it transported me back to the day. The echoey sounds of the crowded gym and the feel of the metal bleachers were the same at that moment as they had been months ago in Teawood High's gym. I bit my lower lip to keep from stirring up the emotions to go along with the memory.

Rick saw what talking about this was doing to me and he gently placed his hand on top of mine.

"London," he whispered, this time softer. "I'm so sorry that I hurt you. It was wrong."

"Why are you doing this now? Here?" I slowly removed my hand from under his but graduated to gnawing on my lower lip. "Months have gone by without so much as an explanation to me. And now that you see me with another guy you wanna be sorry about something? Do you think I'm stupid?"

My shortness of breath and quivering voice betrayed the bold look on my face.

"Maybe it took me seeing you with that dude to make me realize the mistake I'd made," he said like he just read the liner notes off some R & B crooner's CD. All that was left for him to say was "Please, baby, pleeeaze!"

Hmmph. Please.

"Listen, I don't know what to tell you." I looked him squarely in the eyes. "I don't trust anything you say, and it's too late for that anyway."

After a line like that I knew my exit had to be smooth and deliberate. I grabbed my coat, which was lying between us, and stood up to leave. Just as I took the first step, Rick grabbed my hand.

He held it strong enough to stop me in my tracks, but soft enough for it to seem affectionate. When I turned around he was still sitting down but facing me. I tugged my hand but he tightened his grip on it. Tugging any harder would draw unwanted attention to this scene. I can't stand causing scenes. In fact, I hate getting into confrontations primarily for the scenes they cause.

"I can't blame you for how you feel." Rick's eyes were dark brown pools of remorse. "I don't even expect you to forgive me or take me back." My anxiety was a curse that turned me into a statue. "But I wouldn't be able to live with myself knowing that I haven't said sorry." The only thing on the move seemed to be my racing heart.

After those words—and as if in slow motion—Rick brought the back of my hand to his lips and softly kissed it. His eyes kept vigil on my face as he slightly bent his head down to meet my hand. Just then, Brent came to mind. The thought broke the statue curse—but only from the neck up—and I turned my head in search of him. Brent was under a statue curse of his own. He was limply holding his camera with both hands and staring at Rick and me.

He saw the hand kiss.

Ten

I snatched my hand back from Rick with the quickness.

Even though I felt like panicking, I stepped around Rick without so much as a word and made my way off the bleachers. I met up with Brent by the water fountain. In an effort to seem as unaffected as possible by my Rick run-in, I smiled extra wide when I saw Brent.

"Hey," I greeted him. "That was some game, huh?"

"Yeah." Brent stopped and faced me. There was a little tension between us now. "And I think I got in some great shots."

"I can't wait to see 'em," I continued enthusiastically.

We stood there face-to-face for a few heartbeats before we started walking out of the gym together.

As we headed to the Ave, I tried not to go over in my head what had happened. But it was just so random and unexpected that I couldn't help thinking about it.

After the kiss Rick had loosened his grip on my hand. I'd walked away without saying a word to him. In a millisecond I could've sworn I saw the look in his eyes go from sorrowful to smug.

It didn't matter if he was sincere or not. There was nothing he could say or do at this point. I wasn't so sure Rick hadn't already succeeded in doing what he'd wanted to do. By the time Brent and I walked through the front door of the school, it was apparent that that jerk had messed with the easygoing vibe between us.

The crowds of kids hanging out in front of the school and the cars bumping bass kept us busy. Brent nodded greetings to a few guys as we walked by. The only person he stopped to talk to was another silent artsy type we ran into by the front gates.

"What's crackin'?" the guy asked Brent.

"Nuttin' much." Brent and his friend

exchanged the half-hug/half-shake greeting. When they stepped away from each other, Brent started the introductions. "London, this is my boy Seth. We go way back like bendy ballerinas."

"That was corny, man—I'm impressed." Seth laughed. "London, don't let this guy outshine you."

"Trust me, *I'm* the reigning cornball and I ain't letting no one take my crown," I chimed in with a faux attitude, relieved that someone was easing some of the pressure from our emotional tires.

Brent let out an easy laugh.

"Don't make me pull out my list of favorite movies to put y'all to shame." Brent took his backpack off his shoulder and unzipped the front pocket, pretending to search for the list.

"No, we believe you, man." Seth played along.

"I thought so." Brent puffed up his chest like a tough nerd. "Catch you later, man."

We chuckled for a few paces, but then we grew silent again.

On our walk to the juice bar, Rick's hand kiss transformed itself into an elephant moseying down the street in between Brent and me. I tried to act as casual as possible, but something about Brent was different.

"Seth seems like a cool guy," I said. "In a corny way."

Brent smiled. "I like your friends, too," he said. "Pam and Jake are cool people."

I smiled back. A few more awkward seconds passed and then he said, "I didn't get to meet your *other* friend at the game."

No need to ask what friend he meant.

"Uh, he's not really a friend." I was caught off guard and it showed.

"Word?" Brent looked down at his white shell-toe Adidas. "Then he's *more* than a friend?"

I hadn't meant for him to take it that way.

"No," I said quickly. "He's less than a friend. He's an ex-boyfriend."

In my attempt to distance myself from Rick by saying "an ex" instead of "my ex," I ended up making it seem like I'd had a slew of exes. At least that's how it sounded to me. Maybe I was overanalyzing things.

"Oh."

We took a few more paces in silence.

"So it looked like you guys are working on getting back together."

Oh no, time to run some damage control. I didn't want Brent to think I was a playa.

"That is not gonna happen," I assured him. "He dumped me for a more popular girl a few months ago in the worst, most public way possible. And even though we're in one class together, he's never had much to say to me until today. And by coincidence, it's the first time he's seen me with another guy."

"Oh, it's like that, huh?" Mist puffed out of Brent's mouth into the cold air. "So he assumed you and I were a couple?" he asked, obviously amused by it all.

"Yeah, even though Rick and I didn't look nearly as cozy as you and Kelly did the other day." Now I was enjoying myself too.

"So a hand kiss isn't something you'd classify as cozy?"

He got me with that one.

Before I could think of a comeback, Brent reached out and laced his fingers through mine. He stopped walking and gently pulled me to face him. The glow from the streetlamp above our heads softened Brent's expression.

"Then how would you classify a kiss on the lips?"

I was too lost in the moment to answer. As Brent took a slow step closer to me, he reached for my other hand and held it. The nearness of his face warmed mine right up. When his lips finally pressed against mine in a gentle kiss, my entire body felt like summertime.

Eleven

Things were looking up.

A few months ago when I was feeling jilted, no one could've convinced me that I would be head over heels for a great guy, or that Rick would come crawling back. Plus I, of all people, am in a modeling contest!

Life had become so unexpected and I was loving it.

"I've been waiting for you to come home," Mom greeted me just as I walked upstairs. "Congratulations on making it to the fourth week of the contest!"

"Did Pam call to tell you that?" I asked, wondering how my mother was up on the info like CNN. When I found out about my advancement a few days ago, I didn't tell anyone but Pam.

"No." She rolled her eyes. "I went online and checked the site. Darling, you make a stunning Ma-ri-aaa!" She sang out "Maria"—with the rolled *r*—Broadway-style.

This is the same woman who never went on my school website to check out my game stats. The same woman who barely even glanced at my game schedule that was posted at eye level on the fridge door.

"I love how the readers are being so supportive of you." She pumped her fists as she said this. Mom's enthusiasm had now reached hand-aerobics level. "It's the sweet-est thing!"

. . . the same woman who had to be reminded over and over again when the volleyball season ended. My train of thought refused to get off this track. I got the sense that Mom was hoping the Teawood Warriors didn't make state this year so it could all be over quicker. That would mean less time feigning inter-est and a break from picking me up from evening practices.

Since the start of this modeling com-petition, I'd seen a spark reignite in my mother. All of a sudden she was personally interested in one of her kids' extracurricular activities. Dare I say it? She was excited. The polite spectator who offered mild support and lukewarm cheeriness for my volleyball victories was full-on excited about this.

I'd forgotten that look in her eye. That wild imagination that caused her pupils to double in size. She was envisioning the future and she liked the scenario that was playing out in her mind. Maybe she was imagining me on the cover of a fashion magazine. Or possibly starring in a commercial with a catchy retro jingle. All of this would be something forgivable. But if I knew my mother and recognized that look in her eyes correctly, she was visualizing one-upping Kelly's mother. Or she was daydreaming about the praise and envious stares she'd receive from other moms from the child-star circuit.

After years away from the scene, Mom had picked up exactly where she'd left off. She hadn't missed a beat. Standing there with her in that state, I was even starting to experience that same choking sensation I used to feel before each "go-see." My throat would feel like it was slowly closing. When

I'd tell my mother about my struggle to breathe, she'd brush it off as a slight case of the nerves.

Come to think of it, I was more nervous about letting her down than about facing the audition judges.

"This is gonna be great!" She was following me as I walked down the hall to my room. "Where are they asking you to meet up next?"

I was hesitant to tell her, so I went on the defensive.

"Why are you making such a big deal about all this?" Stalling tactic aside, I really wanted to know.

"Can't a mother be excited that her daughter is getting a shot at something so amazing?" she asked, hand on her heart for sympathetic effect.

"I'm just asking because you've never taken such an active interest in my volleyball games."

"I'm proud of your volleyball playing—you know that. It's just that I don't know enough about sports to really jump into that scene with both feet."

"I'm sure Michael Phelps's mother didn't know much about swimming when he started, but you couldn't tell that by looking at her." That was the best example I could come up with on the spot.

"London, you're taking this way over the top." Her hand was now on her hip—the posture she assumes when pulling rank. "I don't know why you're getting so touchy about this. I thought you were having fun with this contest."

"Whatever, Mom." I turned away from her and stepped into my room. "You wouldn't understand anyway."

"Understand what?" The frustration in her voice was up a notch. "Am I missing something or weren't you the one who signed up for this contest on your own?"

My response came in the form of an exasperated exhale.

"Answer me that, London. Why did you audition for a modeling contest that you don't even want to talk about?"

Now she was hitting a nerve.

"The pathetic truth is, I signed up just to meet the cute photo intern working the contest. I didn't do it for me and some desire to be a model, that's for sure." I faced her with my arms crossed tightly across my midsection. "Just like you didn't do it for me when you put me in *all* those castings, even though you *knew* how uncomfortable it made me."

The second it was all out, I regretted saying it. My mom's face fell like the weight of my words was stacked on top of her head. Her eyes blinked away the last ounce of enthusiasm they'd held. Without saying a word, she left my room and gently closed the door behind her.

Twelve

"Welcome to week four of the competition," said Monica, the judge who had detected the shadiness between Kelly and me.

The six contestants left in this competition included Maya, the pixie gal I was fond of. She was impressing voters with her quiet storm of a presence. In person she was an understated beauty, but when the lens was pointed at her, she performed like Sasha Fierce. She and I exchanged smiles once in a while, and the few times I was dumb enough to greet the other contestants, she was the only one to offer me any eye contact. Even though we didn't acknowledge it, there was an unspoken affiliation there. But far be it from me to have formed some type of alliance with her. If I learned anything from my mom's horror stories about Mrs. Fletcher (Kelly's mom), it was not to trust anyone in the entertainment business.

The other girls still in the game were the Rachel Zoe set who half the time couldn't bother to take off their sunglasses indoors. But in their effort to please the judges, they oozed false sincerity. One of them actually asked me the time—but just as Asha walked in the room and noticed her.

"We've invited you back to Chic Boutique on a Friday night because in this week's challenge, you will be judged for your style and presentation of the boutique's collection." Asha's torso stretched higher from her seat than the other two judges'. They were seated behind the customer service counter, just as they had been during the very first week of the competition. When she said "presentation," she paused to give me a head-to-toe glare. Because this was an after-store-hours meeting, I had just come from my volleyball game. I hadn't had time to change into a stylista after my shower. The powers that be at school were cracking down on after-game loiterers, so they cleared the girls' locker room pretty quickly.

If Asha was disappointed with the school-girl argyle sweater and worn-in pair of cords that I'd thrown on, I wondered what she would have said had she seen my usual postgame attire. She should have counted herself lucky I left my smelly gym bag in my locker.

I was starting to accept the fact that Asha was never going to dig me. We started off on the wrong foot and I'd been letting her down ever since. She never really verbally slammed me or anything. It was just the disapproving looks that she threw me. It was actually kind of funny in a modeling-contest-judge spoof kind of way. Pam had grown to love my Asha imitation. Every time she said something overly dramatic, I fluttered my eyelids, tensed up my jaw, and pointed my chin in her direction.

"Everyone will be paired up into teams of two." Didier took over with his commanding voice and level eye contact. "But each of you will work independently in styling a fabulous fall look for your partner, which she will in turn model. In the end, you'll be judged on both your fashion sense and your modeling skills."

Didier beamed at the end of his instructions, obviously eager to see how the evening would play out.

Monica picked up the writing pad in front of her. "As soon as I call out who you'll be paired with, you'll have fifteen minutes to select a look—accessories included—after which, you will meet your partner in designated fitting rooms to help put the look together. The first name I call in the pair is the person who will model their partner's looks first."

I was trying to keep track of all the details and instructions they were throwing at us. I didn't even catch the new gleam in Monica's eyes every time she looked my way. It was possible that I was just being paranoid in thinking that she'd witnessed what appeared to be a crush triangle among Kelly, Brent, and me. I shook it off and listened closely for my name to be called. She didn't—until the very end.

"And the last duo will be Kelly and London," Monica called out, her eyes dancing as she said my name.

Didier walked over to the contestants and handed a pink index card to each of us. On the card he handed me were Kelly's dress, top, bottom, jeans, and shoe sizes. I guess they seriously wanted me to shop for Kelly of all people.

I've watched enough reality shows to know that producers will choreograph dramatic scenes by placing two known enemies in the ring together. This pairing was no mistake. Monica knew that Kelly and I had history and she wanted to toss things up and see what jumped off.

I was not going to give her and the other judges that satisfaction.

The contestants scattered throughout the store in search of clothing items that would complement their stylista visions within the fifteen minutes. I didn't take more than two paces before the accessories fixture caught my eye. Most of the selections were bright colored. It reminded me of the retro eighties look from classic Cyndi Lauper videos. It was stuff Pam would wear with one of her candy-colored pairs of jeans and favorite Pastry sneakers.

Then I eyed a silvery bird pendant hanging on a simple, long silver necklace. I grabbed it before anyone else could—not that anyone was close by. The other girls— including Kelly—were leafing through clothing racks in a frenzy. They were all obviously saving the accessories for last. But this pendant necklace wooed me enough to work the other way around. I didn't know if I was doing the right thing but I had no time to think it over. I'd heard of people decorating a room around one pretty lamp. So why not apply the same inspiration to clothes?

A photographer I didn't recognize appeared out of nowhere and pointed her lens at me. She walked around me until she could see what was in my hand.

"Don't get thrown off by the photographers." Didier must've seen my reaction. "We're documenting this part of the challenge as well." I looked around and saw two other photographers following other contestants. *Great*. I inwardly panicked. *Now my secret will really get let out the bag.*

I focused on not looking so confused. This week's challenge would separate the real from the phonies—and as I was so acutely aware, I was one big phony.

I'd made it this far off "alluring" vibes and reader support, but this week would spotlight my total lack of fashion sensibilities. I knew nothing about style. If I could live in my volleyball uniform, I would. It was thrilling to wear shorts without being laughed at, so yes, wearing my uniform booty shorts every day would suit me just fine.

The only way out of this would be to channel my inner Pam. What would she do in this situation? What would she pair up with this pendant?

I walked in circles around the same three skirt fixtures and still nothing came to mind. *Click!* went the camera pointed at me. From the corner of my eye, I saw a speed-walking Kelly pass by in a blur. She had a few articles of clothing folded over her arm. Now was a good time to panic.

"Ten minutes left, ladies," Asha called out the nerve-racking reminder. It made me feel like they were breathing down my neck.

I decided to stop circling the three fixtures and moved on to tops. That was when I saw the perfect blouse—it was a vintage Victorian satiny blouse with short capped sleeves and a high neck, which would make it perfect for a low-hanging necklace. The color was perfect—a slate blue-gray always goes great with silver. I grabbed the size small [*Click!*] and moved on. Not heading to any location in particular, I thought the important thing was just to keep moving.

As I made a beeline to the opposite side of the room, a skirt that was on that trio of fixtures I had been circling came to mind. I did an about-face and this time walked with a destination in mind. On my way there, I stopped to pick up a pair of black ankle boots that Pam had been gushing about. "Those go with any look" I remembered her raving. I was stalled looking for the right size for Kelly. *Click!*

"Five minutes, everyone." Asha would be great on a movie set.

The skirt I'd had in mind turned out to have suspenders attached, so I couldn't use that one. Instead of freaking out [*Click!*], I leafed through the neighboring rack in search of a similarly shaped balloon skirt. I found a high-waisted pencil skirt. *Click!* I wasn't crazy about the look of the waist, but the skirt was the length I was looking for. Plus it had pockets that would create a more hour-glass figure.

I looked at the items one more time. The look didn't feel complete. I rushed back to the accessories fixtures and picked up a wide black belt. The buckle was a shiny silver, which went back to the necklace's theme. Next, I picked up a pair of silver studs. *Click!* My mom always told me that large necklaces shouldn't compete with large earrings and vice versa.

"One minute!" This time it was Monica who did the honors. Asha was probably midgulp on her coffee.

I got startled like someone had just snuck behind me and shouted, "Boo!" *Click!* My heart was thumping as I reviewed my items and asked myself if there was anything else I could bring. Just to be on the safe side, I grabbed a silver cuff with a blue center stone, a black toile clutch purse, and gray knit beanie. *Click! Click! Click!*

"Time!" Asha resumed her duties. I breathed in like I had just emerged from underwater. I hadn't realized that I had been practically holding my breath those last few seconds.

But I did it. I picked out an entire look in the time given. We were directed to place our selections on three clothing racks. There was one shoe bag per person for us to drop the footwear in. Kelly and I were to share the same rack. Our individual selections were separated by a long blue garment bag.

Even though I didn't make eye contact with Kelly, I did manage to sneak a peek at her selections for me. They were much different from mine. She'd chosen warm fall colors—burgundy and brown—while I'd chosen the cold tones of blue and gray. I immediately doubted my selections. I wondered if I had veered way off into untrendy zone. I wouldn't know a trend if it gave me a tetanus shot, so I wasn't sure if my selections would be seen as way off.

To get a second opinion, I looked over at the two other clothing racks. Pixie and her partner seem to have acted on the same wavelength. They both had chosen clothes you'd wear to go out clubbin'. Dark blue jeans were the foundation for both outfits. Their selections didn't confirm or deny my sinking suspicions about my outdated choices. The girls on the other rack seemed to have selected more than one outfit each. I wasn't sure if wearing both a dress and pants were what was hot in the streets, but it seemed like the amount of items exceeded what one girl was able to wear. It was as if some of the contestants had used their fifteen minutes to go two rounds of clothing searches.

I caught myself attempting to judge how well the other girls would do in this week's challenge. I would never have tried to make such a judgment call in the contest's earlier weeks. Something in me had definitely changed. I was putting my more competitive face forward. No longer just in it for the thrill, I told myself that I'd try my best to survive this week. Things had been going well so far, but I didn't want to count my eggs before they were hatched. This week's challenge was tougher than I'd expected it would be.

Kelly stood in silence next to me. We both looked straight ahead at our selections, while the other paired-up contestants whispered cordially to each other.

The judges were in a semihuddle, distracted by the logistics they'd written out. At that moment, the lead photographer emerged from downstairs. Brent was close behind him. Tiny butterfly wings tickled my stomach when I saw him. Brent and I made brief eye contact and offered a very subtle smile to each other as if to say hey. Since the kiss, we'd been texting each other back and forth. Nothing deep. Just some sweet hellos and a few LOL-worthy comments.

The lead photographer signaled to Didier that everything down there was set up. They were ready to get crackin'.

"Okay, two of you will have to follow me downstairs to the changing room and photo shoot area," Didier announced as if addressing a nonexistent person in the back of the room when the rest of us were standing only a few feet away from him.

Despite his authoritative announcement, Didier didn't know which two people that would be. He searched Monica's and Asha's faces for help.

"Why don't we start with Kelly and London," Monica offered. From the look on her face, I could tell she was proud of her problem-solving skills.

"*Très bien.*" I loved it when my BFF spoke French. He used it sparingly so as not to play it out. "Ladies, if you would please follow me to your makeshift dressing area. Brent will bring your items down on the elevator."

Kelly and I took our first steps at the same time. She didn't want to be the one to tag behind and neither did I. We walked shoulder to shoulder. When I quickened my pace to take the lead, she attempted to do the same.

I wondered how obvious this was to everyone else. We were in a race, but neither of us wanted to be transparent about it by speed walking. We also couldn't step too fast or we would clip the back of Didier's shoes. Didier had that brisk Manhattan stride down, so we easily managed to keep him from becoming a casualty of our ridiculousness.

The path to the "Employees Only" door had been cleared so we weren't forced to walk to it single file. A few quick paces later, a few clothing rounders dotted the pathway. Kelly and I split up on either sides of the clearance rounder. Since Kelly would end up a bit closer to the door, I took a wide, quick step so as not to lose ground once I cleared the rounder. When we were walking side by side again, Kelly was ahead by a half a pace. She would most likely be the first to get to the door.

Didier pulled the heavy door open and held it there. He turned and graciously asked us to step through and meet him at the bottom of the stairs. Kelly walked in first. Although I didn't end up being the last one through (Didier was), it still bugged me that I was behind Kelly.

Once downstairs, Didier then took the lead, ushering us through a long hallway. After we passed the break room, we got to the bright open space where the cameras and lights were set up. Jazz music was playing on a low volume.

"Your fitting room is a shared one right there," Didier said, pointing to a white door with plantation shutters at the far corner of the room. The clothing rack was already parked in front of that door.

We sweetly thanked Didier and headed for the room.

It was a relatively large fitting room, so I rolled the rack in there. There were floor-to-ceiling mirrors and clothing hooks along the walls, as well as a seating area.

I exhaled. Now was the time Kelly and I would have to set aside our differences and work together. After removing the ankle boots from the plastic bag, I faced Kelly.

"Hey." I greeted her as if this was the first time I was seeing her. It was better than nothing. "Here's what I selected for you."

"Okay." Kelly finally addressed me, but it was through the mirror instead of directly to my face. She had already tossed off her shoes and it seemed like she was ready to get to the business of modeling. I felt relieved that she was also deciding to lean on her professionalism to get through this awkward moment.

"Once you throw on the skirt and top, I'll style the accessories." I couldn't believe the words that were coming out of my mouth. I never pictured myself styling anyone. It felt good knowing that I had a look in mind that I could bring to life. I got a slice of understanding for what Pam loves to do.

While Kelly was changing, I started gathering the accessories tangled around a spare hanger. Catching my reflection in the mirror made me proud. I was keeping busy, and it was giving me the perfect distraction I needed. All day while I was at school, I had been sulking over last night's stupid argument with my mom. She'd left for work before I got up this morning, so I hadn't seen her since she walked out of my room last night. I knew I had to call or text her to apologize but I didn't. And the longer I was putting it off, the more I felt guilty and haunted by it. But ever since I walked into Chic Boutique tonight, I hadn't been thinking about the argument or the guilt.

"What's next?" Kelly asked, staring at herself in the mirror. She bent over to adjust the boots on her feet.

The blouse and skirt fit her nicely. So far, so good.

I handed her the wide belt. "Here you go," I told her. The look was coming together better than I imagined. Kelly was already looking ready to parade down the city streets and stand out in a crowd of fashionistas.

I wasn't sure I felt comfortable enough putting the accessories on for her, so I handed them to Kelly one by one. The earrings. The pendant necklace. The cuff bracelets. I had to help her clasp the bracelets. When she held out her arm, I stood as far from her personal space as possible. When that was done, I stepped back and took a look at her in the mirror. She adjusted the necklace because it was caught in her hair, but that's all she did. She allowed herself to strictly play the role of model.

I knew that I would be judged for the way Kelly wore the look. So in my stylista mode, I studied the way the clothes lay on her.

I looked at her both through the mirror and directly. The tiny lace trim of the blouse's neck was slouching so I reached out and stood it up. Next I noticed that the necklace clasp was showing, so as gingerly and respectfully as possible, I moved it out of sight to the back of her neck.

Her boots had been folded over, so I bent down and put the flaps upright. When I stood up, I studied Kelly's look again.

"Can you adjust your skirt to get the pockets to lie right on your hips?" I asked.

Kelly took a pinchful of the skirt on each side and twisted the skirt into place. "Can you smooth down the pockets by putting your hands in them?" I'd noticed that bumps had now formed at her hips. Kelly obliged.

This was going great. Kelly and I actually made an okay team.

"One last thing," I told her as I walked to the hook where the cable-knit beanie was hanging. "Let's see how this tops off the whole look."

Wordlessly, Kelly put the beanie on her head in a nondescript way. It was just sitting on the top of her head and didn't look right.

I had seen Pam's cousin Layla wear hats

like this a few times and I loved the way she rocked them.

"Mind if I just show you how I want it worn?" I asked Kelly, before removing the beanie and laying it down toward the back of her head. "I'm just gonna put most of your hair in it and leave your bangs out." I wanted to give her a heads-up before I made any sudden, unexpected moves.

Although Kelly was being cooperative and playing the professional model role, it was clear that she didn't want to cross that line and style herself on my behalf. She may not have wanted to be caught giving me push back but she certainly wasn't going to bend over backward just to keep up her falsely sweet reputation in this competition.

Once I wrangled her thick curls into the beanie, I lightly finger combed the wispy strands in front of her head so that the right amount of hair peaked out. After I was done, I stepped back to examine Kelly's reflection. The bean was a very Katie Holmes touch. When I did that I caught a slight look of surprise on her face. Kelly liked her look, but she didn't tell me. I had to admit it to myself—the girl looked amazing in the

outfit I'd picked. I loved the womanly silhouette of the skirt and blouse. The beanie
tied everything together nicely and gave
Kelly the look of a sophisticated stylista.

Pam would be so proud.

"Not bad for a contest plant," Kelly
uttered under her breath just as I was beaming at my work.

"What's that?" I thought she said what I
heard, but I wanted to make sure.

"Just that you've come a long way for
someone who was selected as a contest
plant."

I gave her a blank stare, too offended to
speak. I wasn't sure what a "contest plant"
was but I knew it wasn't good.

"You know," Kelly started, "when someone like you gets picked for something
like this, the judges usually expect her to
phase out right away. It's just important
to them that an underqualified person gets
in, otherwise they'd be called elitist and
exclusionary."

Kelly eyed my reflection up and down.

"Wow, well, whatever makes you feel
better about yourself," I heard myself say.
My heart was pounding because this clas-
sified as a confrontation. I just wanted her

to shut up and go out there for her photo shoot. She was being crazy offensive and I wanted her out of my sight.

"I think they're ready for you out there," I told her.

The jazz music was still playing softly and the photo crew was joking around with one another and chatting. I heard Brent's shy laugh. Didier hadn't knocked on our door yet asking us to come out, but I was sure he wouldn't mind us being a tad early on the scene.

"Just because you're styling me on this round, doesn't mean you can tell me what to do." Kelly was really looking for a fight. I couldn't believe she was carrying on like this.

"Whatever, Kelly," I repeated. "Why don't you just grow up?"

"I'll grow up right after you and your delusional ass get a clue." She finally looked directly at me. The fact that she was dressed to the nines yet was spitting venom in a steady, subdued voice made her seem even more psychotic.

"Delusional?" The girl was going overboard.

"You heard me," she folded her arms over

the blouse and I was afraid she would wrinkle it. "You're a sloppy, unpolished, and unpretty jock who somehow landed in this contest thinking that you belong here. Everybody knows you're addicted to competition. It doesn't matter if it's on the court or on a walkway, you'll take your high any way you can get it. And now you're here acting like you know how to style somebody when all you wear is gym clothes every damn day."

Kelly's words hit me like a ton of bricks. *Is that how people view me?* It was like she had crawled into my head and dug up my insecurities and handed them to me on a silver platter.

This must have been how my mom felt when Kelly's mom double-crossed her. It was like I was caught using the front entrance at Kelly's elite country club when I was the help who was restricted to the servants' entrance. I suddenly felt like her royal handmaiden standing there primping her highness in the fitting room. That realization felt like a cold bucket of water dumped over my head. The iciness of it obviously short circuited my response wiring because I said nothing. My silence prompted Kelly to continue her triflin' tirade.

"Not to mention, you're delusional if you think that the intern photographer is seriously interested in you." Kelly went there. "It's just too bad for him you're just using him to get insider contest info that could cost him his job."

That sounded like a threat. Did Kelly figure out what Brent told me?

"Hold up—who the hell do you think you are?" I finally shot back.

"I'm the only person brave enough to tell you the truth. You are making a fool out of yourself here, London. The people voting for you online are only doing that for their amusement. They don't want to pull themselves away from a train wreck. And from one girl to another—you're wasting your time with Brent. A guy who works with gorgeous models and sophisticated women won't look twice at you. If it's your mom making you do this, tell her you're not cut out for it."

That was enough. The last ounce of calm in me flew out the window. I don't know what floored me more—the fact that she had dared to insult me or the fact that a small part of me believed what she said.

"You conceited little witch," I snapped. "You are so full of yourself! You think you can coast on your looks and everyone's gonna get out of your way? Well, I'm here to tell you—that's not the way this works!" My chest was heaving and I was shouting at this point. All of the angst that I'd been holding in all day just exploded. I wanted to knock that beanie right off Kelly's head with one clean punch. I'd never punched another person before—if you don't count the odd wayward fist on the court.

She'd just insulted everything that I stood for. And right to my face and in a way no different from an anchorwoman reading the top news headlines.

When my anger boiled to the top, it took shape as tears and welled up in my eyes. Kelly's smarmy expression started to look fuzzy to me.

"This contest doesn't mean as much to me as it does to you because this is all you got going for yourself. I don't have to put up with this!" I shouted loud enough for the whole floor to hear.

With that, my wobbly legs carried me to the fitting room door, which I swung open like a force of nature. I stopped short when I saw Didier, Brent, and the rest of the photo crew staring at me in wide-eyed shock.

Then it clicked that they'd heard everything I'd yelled to Kelly, but hadn't heard what Kelly had said to me, because she'd said it in a low voice.

Just then, Kelly stepped out, giving everyone her best rendition of a devastated damsel. The one who ended up looking like the diva was me. And no one had love for a diva and her outbursts.

"I just need a minute and I'll be right there," she said to Didier in a little, wounded voice. I was wrong about Kelly's lack of talent. The girl's a great actress and is a mastermind at all things devious. She obviously had planned to screw me and I'd played right into her hands.

Didier looked concerned for poor Kelly. "Are you okay?" He followed her into the fitting room, rushing past me without so much as a glance.

Brent looked mad disappointed and surprised. There was nothing more I could do or say at this point. I walked off the set and headed upstairs and then out of Chic Boutique.

I planned on not ever returning.

Thirteen

I felt so angry after Kelly got all brand-new on me, I had to walk it out like DJ Unk.

The air outside was a bit frosty. I buttoned up my waistcoat and pulled up the collar to block the chilly wind. Unfortunately, I had to walk against the wind to get home. But I was determined to endure the fifteen minutes it took to get there. I just wanted to lock myself in my room. It was the second night in a row that I'd had those plans. Just yesterday I'd woken up feeling like I was on top of the world.

The time on my cell said 7:06. My dad was scheduled to pick me up from Chic Boutique a little after 8 p.m. I flipped open my phone and texted him that I was already on my way home. A few seconds later, he texted back *K. Hope you had a great day.*

My dad knew exactly what was up between my mom and me. Knowing him, he wouldn't get involved unless I took too long to apologize. Sometimes I wish my dad wasn't so levelheaded. It's like the man can't relate to any type of deviation from the straight and narrow. It makes me feel like a malfunctioning robot sometimes.

On the walk home, I passed only a few pedestrians. There was a stillness to the neighborhood. I was wearing rubber-soled shoes, so my feet barely made a sound hitting the pavement. There weren't even that many cars on the road. The moon was full and luminous. And when the wind picked up, it just swirled all the stillness from miles around.

Even though I had just had my public outburst, I was feeling very calm. A visible cloud of mist puffed out of my mouth when I exhaled. I turned off the main road and passed a row of mismatched houses—tall brick homes, low-roofed ranches, classic colonials, spacious front porches, small manicured lawns, and large front yards. Some houses seemed dark and lifeless inside, while the windows of others reflected a warm glow of light.

The stillness followed me home. My dad's car wasn't in the driveway. Aside from the light on on the front porch, everything seemed dark. As soon as I got inside, I switched on the living room lights.

No one was home. That's when I remembered my parents had planned to take the boys to a movie. I was glad that I didn't have to face anyone tonight, but a small part of me had been hoping to see them so that I could feel normal again. I didn't want to be reminded that a lot had changed. I was now this modeling, stylist diva who breaks out with outbursts. Or was I? Maybe I was a delusional phony who got mixed up in a world I knew nothing about.

I wasn't sure anymore.

To add injury to insult, Brent had witnessed the whole thing. He and I had just shared our first kiss and now it looked like whatever we were working on was going to be stalled indefinitely. I didn't want to face him and I wasn't sure he was invested enough to deal with me, considering what he overheard.

I thought back to the day I saw him

in Art Attack. He was minding his own business and I inserted myself into his life. I couldn't remember the last time I was that pushy. Maybe I was experiencing some kind of delayed posttraumatic stress syndrome.

All of these thoughts bombarded me as I lay on my bed and stared at the ceiling. After tussling with my confusion and going over the last few crazy events, I drifted off into a deep sleep.

I woke up in the middle of the night from a crazy dream that I couldn't remember. It was 3 a.m. I turned on my computer and started typing a draft e-mail to the judges. It was a letter of apology for skipping out. I didn't offer an explanation, only a condemnation of my actions and a promise to come back a stronger candidate, should I be fortunate enough to stay. Now that I had cooled down, I could see the foulness of my earlier behavior. Even if I didn't belong in this competition, I didn't want to pull a Robert Muraine of *So You Think You Can Dance* fame and bow out before my time in the contest was up. Besides, quitting was just not my style.

After clicking send, I was able to drift back to a more peaceful sleep.

This was the first Saturday in weeks that I would be at work for my full eight-hour shift. My manager was happy to see me when I walked in bright and early. I'd left the house early that morning and decided to eat my breakfast at the small park around the corner from work.

"London, can I talk to you for a second?" he asked me in the break room a few minutes before the store was set to open.

"Sure," I told him.

He looked like he'd just woken up a few minutes earlier. His lips were cracked and he still had tiny bits of crust in the corners of his eyes. I took a step back in case he was about to set off a yawn. I had just dumped what was left of my hot chocolate, so I leaned against the sink.

"You've been missing a lot of Saturdays in the past month," he started. *Uh-oh*, I thought. *Was I about to lose my job?* I still needed about half of my summer camp tuition.

The gamble I took by signing up for the modeling contest to get to know Brent was not working out in my favor at all. I was neglecting what was important. I would end up with nothing that I started out hoping for—not my sports camp money, my job, or Brent.

"I've been trying to make up for it by filling in for other people whenever possible," I reminded him in my last-ditch effort to save my job.

"That's true and I appreciate that," he continued. "So I was thinking that I would instead have you on the schedule as a floater. That way you don't have to worry about skipping more Saturdays and I can have the peace of mind knowing that other employees can be covered when there's a last-minute change of plans."

In volleyball terms, there's a name for the player who serves as a kind of team floater. The position is called libero and it's the only one where the player wears a different uniform than the rest. They look and act different from the other players. That was me—the libero at work and the libero-looking contestant.

"But I most likely won't be missing any more Saturdays," I explained, thinking about my dropping out of the contest. Even if I did go back to the contest, there was only one more week left.

"You say that now, but what if the contest needs you to commit to a few more?" he asked. "Or what if you win and they need you to tour France or something?" Boss man was being over-the-top now. "You never know," he responded to the expression on my face. "Look, London, I don't want to lose you around here, but I think this is the best way to go from here—at least until things calm down a bit."

There was nothing more I could say. He had considered his options and his mind was made up. I couldn't blame him. I had been unreliable these past few Saturdays. He had accommodated me up until now.

"Thanks for working with me on this," I told him. "I realize that there've been a lot of changes and I wouldn't want to lose this job over it."

"Neither would I," he assured me.

Fourteen

Thankfully, I was pulled off register when my goth coworker's shift started two hours later. I stepped away unscathed from any transaction dilemmas that could've plagued my morning.

It was a slow enough day that I was able to text Pam back and forth a few times. She was visiting family in Brooklyn and wouldn't be able to meet me for lunch that day. She texted me some words of encouragement and sent me a funny photo of her at the Caribbean marketplace, standing next to a barrelful of yellow plantains, her favorite food. I smiled at the look of ecstasy on her face as she clutched a few of them in her arms, lookin' like Alicia Keys after the Grammys.

Pam always knew how to make me smile when life seemed like it was getting too serious.

But every time my phone vibrated, I half-expected, half-hoped that it would be Brent texting me. He hadn't so much as left a comment on my Facebook page since my outburst. I was too embarrassed to contact him. Anyway, his silence was probably a sign that he was as much a loser user as Rick was.

The moment when I came out of the fitting room and saw the look on his face replayed in my mind.

"Excuse me," a guy said as I was about to start stocking colored pencils. Since starting this job, I'd spent more time stocking that fixture than anything else in the store. It was amazing how fast those bitties flew off the shelves. I turned to the source of the voice.

"Yes, may I help you?" I asked, happy to get off my knee and stretch my legs.

When I looked up, I was caught *completely* off guard. That "customer" was none other than Rick. He was the last person I expected or wanted to see. But I kept those feelings to myself.

"Hi," he started cautiously. "I'm looking

for a few colored pencils for my little brother. Do they come in a pack at all or do I have to buy them as singles?"

"There's this pack right here." I reached for the box of twenty pencils on the shelf right below my shoulder and handed it to him with as much emotion as a robot.

"Oh!" Rick chuckled sheepishly. "It's always like that—by the time you ask for help, the thing you're looking for is right under your nose."

"Happens all the time," I deadpanned. "No worries."

I turned my back to him and continued working. I was in no mood. *Maybe he'll just leave now that he's gotten what he supposedly came in for.* But that was wishful thinking.

"London," Rick said under his breath before clearing his throat. The unmistakable sincerity in his tone piqued my curiosity. I didn't turn around, but my restocking pace slowed to a crawl. "Look, I've gotta be straight up. I'm sure you heard—or *will* hear—that homegirl axed me for another dude."

Now, this is getting interesting, I thought, riveted. Only my actions didn't show it.

"But I'm glad it happened because,

number one, I deserved it after how I did you," he continued matter-of-factly. "And number two, I needed it because that *ish* woke me up and made me realize I was smelling myself too hard these past few months."

"London, almost done there?" My manager was at the end of the aisle with a "no fraternizing" scowl on his face.

"Just about," I answered. "I'll be right there." When he walked away, I threw the empty cartons into a container. I was ready to carry off everything in my arms. Rick looked at me expectantly when I faced him, but still I said nothing.

"I just want to say that I'm sorry I messed up what we used to have," he insisted. "I'm not talking about the dating relationship, but about our friendship. And I know I don't deserve to have that anymore, but I wouldn't want my past stupidity to continue causing tension between us. I mean, we have two more years of bumping into each other on a daily basis."

"London." My manager was back. This time he stood there and waited for me.

"Look, this isn't the time or place—," I started.

"What are you doing for lunch? Can we talk then?" he asked. "What time should I be back?"

"Okay, yes. In a half hour." In my haste, I heard myself agreeing before walking away.

Thirty minutes later on the dot, he was back and waiting for me by the exit. I led him to the closest sandwich shop so that we could get the lunch over with quickly.

"Remember the time we doubled up to play beach volleyball against another couple?" Rick reminisced without bringing up our past drama. This relaxed me a bit.

"I'll never forget that dive you took." I giggled in spite of myself. "I've never seen someone take such a mouthful of sand."

"You wouldn't believe how long I was flossing out grains after that." He laughed.

"No!" I cracked up even louder.

"It was all worth it because we kicked ass." He underscored what he said with his talking hands. "I'll team up with you any day, London. You play with heart because you're so competitive."

This hit a nerve. "What do you mean by that?" I demanded. "Why do people peg me for this competition-crazed chick?"

"That's not what I'm saying at all. It's just that you're driven by a good challenge," he explained.

"You don't know everything about me. I do a lot of things just for the fun of it." I didn't sound convincing.

"I'm sure of that," Rick soothed. "Like this modeling thing? I'm sure you decided it would be fun to go to the casting. Just for the *fun* of it," he repeated with a teasing glimmer in his eyes.

I averted my gaze so he wouldn't be able to read me anymore.

Rick and I exchanged a few more funny memories and then I headed back to work. It was oddly enough a pleasant half hour. It felt good not to be angry at him anymore.

I looked at my laptop screen in disbelief. I wouldn't even have checked Facemag.com had it not been for Pam's urgent text message asking me to.

There on the contest update was the rundown of week four's challenge. All the drama was there in writing—including the e-mail that I sent to the judges. I couldn't *believe* they posted my letter word for word. "After storming out of the contest, London saw the error of her ways and sent the judges this apology," I read aloud. Just when I felt I was going to be sick to my stomach, my eyes caught the final stats. Amazingly, and simply by default, I was ranked *number three*! That was right behind Kelly (number 2) and Maya (number 1), which meant I was invited to the competition's final week. I had to read it over just to believe what I'd seen.

Basically, the reason I was chosen was because I was the best out of the worst. Two of the contestants were disqualified for not following the rules. The judges penalized them for picking more than one outfit. It was a big no-no to be suspected of bending the rules or cheating. The extra clothing allowed them to have more chances to get the look right, which wasn't fair to the other contestants.

The fourth-ranked contestant didn't style or model the looks all that well. I was still in the competition because Kelly got rave reviews for the outfit that I styled. She also knocked her photo shoot out the box.

I felt like a cartoon character shaking off some absurd injury that flesh-and-bone people couldn't survive.

Everything was happening at such a

whirlwind pace, I didn't even know what to think. This was superexciting news! Never had I imagined myself getting this far in the modeling competition. It was crazy.

The judges sent out an e-mail asking contestants to report to Chic Boutique bright and early next Saturday morning for the final day of the competition.

As I sat looking at the posted photos of me shopping like I knew what I was doing, I pushed aside the sinking suspicion that Rick and Kelly were somewhat right about my supercompetitive nature. *They think they know me, but they don't.* My passion comes from more than just the idea of winning.

Fifteen

"Gurrrl." Pam dragged out the word in a way that signaled that she had something juicy to tell me.

"What?" I couldn't wait to hear her news. Pam usually knows how to make any story sound like golden gossip. It was clear that Pam was just trying to keep my mind off the MIA Brent, so I didn't make it tough for her. I gave her my full attention.

"My boyfriend is a lunatic," she started. I wondered what could possibly be off about Jake. He was, like, the nicest guy and the sweetest boyfriend to Pam.

"Oh no." I let my concern show. Drama in my own love life was all I could bear.

Pam and Jake couldn't be having relationship trouble—not now.

"Well, he is!" Pam stressed. "His parents flew back to the Philippines for a family wedding, so he and his immature brothers are trying to plan a house party sometime this week. Maybe even tonight."

"Huh?" I was confused. "Why don't they just wait for Friday or Saturday night?"

"Well, 'cause his parents know who they're dealing with and they're coming back Friday morning."

I choked on a chuckle. "That's hilarious."

"Yeah, gurl," she agreed. "And them knuckleheads are trying to enlist me and my fabulous party-planning skills. I will not be an accomplice to a bad plan."

"Why do you think it's a bad plan?"

"For starters, they expect fifty people to be able to party into the wee hours on a weeknight without the neighbors getting suspicious. Their parents have the Filipino community on them like neighborhood watch. Just yesterday I caught their mom's friend cruising by the house."

"Hilarious," I repeated.

"But they're not heeding my warnings because they think I'm being dramatic."

"Well, now, little boy who cried wolf, now that the wolves are really salivating, no one believes you."

"I know." Pam pretended to sob and I put my arm around her for a quick hug.

"There, there," I cooed. "Just think of it this way—you'll get to say 'I told you so' when this is all over."

That made Pam smile.

"Hey, London," Trish, a classmate from my history class, said as she approached us. "Great styling skills. Pam's influence rubbing off on you?"

"Of course, it is, *dahling*!" Pam forgot about her trouble.

"But what I'm dying to know is, what got you so upset that you stormed out on everything?"

I was wondering when that was going to come up. When I checked the site's message boards that morning, a few people were asking the same thing.

"Uh—," I started.

"London had to bounce for personal reasons," a quick-thinking Pam said, beating me to the punch. What would I do without her?

"Oh, word?" Trish was too curious for her own good.

"Word," Pam answered and kept things moving. "Coming to the game at North Side High tonight?" she asked Trish.

"No, but good luck tonight, London." Trish accepted Pam's answer and took her cue to move on. "And good luck this weekend at Chic Boutique."

"Thanks," I finally managed to say.

Once Trish was out of earshot, I told Pam, "I shouldn't have walked out on that competition if I couldn't stand up to the consequences on my own."

"Yeah, well," she said, "you can handle the next one—I promise."

Later that evening, I was in full uniform, ready for our game against North Side High, Kelly's high school in the neighboring town. I was hoping she wouldn't show up to the game, because I was not ready to run into her.

Even though I was excited about the game, a part of me was heartbroken about Brent. He was so enthusiastic about watching me play. That got me wondering, *What if he shows up here tonight?* Like a glutton for disappointment, I scanned the crowd. But, of course, I didn't see him. Sitting near the top of the bleachers were Pam and Jake chatting up a storm, obviously debating the house party idea. While Coach Pat gave our team one extra courtside chat in a huddle, my eyes wandered and landed on Kelly sitting a few rows back. Of all the places to sit as a North Side student, why did she choose the bleachers behind us, the visiting team?

Just then, Rick walked over and took the open spot next to Kelly. Rick had never been much of a Kelly fan, so he didn't say hello to her when he noticed she was nearby. He beamed me a smile and I nodded in acknowledgment.

As I headed to the court, someone two rows behind Rick and Kelly caught my eye. Brent was sitting there, waving to get my attention.

When it was clear to Brent that I was looking at him, he held up a handmade sign that read OLYMPICS 2016 OR BUST.

I smiled in spite of myself. A warm sensation filled my cheeks.

It was just the mental boost I needed right at that moment. I uncrossed my arms, sat up, took a deep breath, and let it out slowly. Brent's sign was a sign. It was encouragement to get right back on the track I had allowed myself to stray from. Not to mention, it was a sign that Brent was as sincere as I originally thought he was. He was here in support of me. I didn't catch his familiar camera bag on or near him. He was here as a friend, not as a photographer. That made me feel even better.

That good feeling was short-lived. As soon as she noticed her good fortune of being seated near ex and future boyfriends, Kelly seized the golden opportunity. She made herself known to both of them. And *then*, in the biggest WTF moment, she introduced Rick to Brent. I wondered what she was saying to them, because she was talking a mile a minute and gesturing to me.

Then it was Rick who took over the conversation. From the way he was smoothing down his invisible goatee and nodding in my direction, I could tell he was posturing—big time. Now he was bumping his fist to his heart and gesturing to me. It didn't take a lip reader to know that Rick was trying to get Brent riled up. I was sure he was bragging that we recently got reacquainted with each other. But there was bound to be some exaggeration in anything he was saying. The showy Rick was back in all his big-headed glory.

Rick's plan appeared to work. Brent's jaw tightened and he lowered the sign he'd made for me.

I sucked in air so fast that I choked on it and started coughing.

"You okay, L?" the team captain asked me.

I wasn't okay. Rick played me again. Just because his relationship failed, he was out to sabotage mine. How could this be happening? I coughed a few more times before clearing my throat.

"I'm fine," I lied.

The whistle blew in the next second and I sprang into action. I punched the ball like it was Rick's face. But the true person I was mad at was myself. I was the one who allowed Rick to take me for this ride, knowing he could not be trusted. I was the one who was gullible.

The passion that I was playing with wasn't a good thing. A few times, I hit the ball so hard, I knocked it out of play.

"C'mon, London," I heard Coach Pat bark. "Focus!"

It was my turn to serve. North Side High's cheerleaders led the crowd in an annoying chant in their effort to break my concentration. I threw the ball in the air, raised my right arm above my head, and swung my balled fist at it, sending the ball straight to . . . the net. I couldn't shake off the betrayal I felt and it was screwing with my game.

"Let's go, London," Pam screamed at the top of her lungs.

For my second serving attempt, I got the ball over the net, but it landed out of play.

"Damn!" I shouted to myself.

The crowd cheered my mistake. My teammates got into position in preparation for North Side's serve.

Our opponents nailed their serve, which kick-started a volley. I managed to hit the ball over when it came to me, but the next time it headed my way, I dove for it and missed. The crowd roared for North Side's point.

Because of my mistakes, we ended up losing that first set.

Coach Pat had me sit out the next set. I've sat out sets before, but never for this reason. It was clear that I'd lost my cool out there and my choices were costing the team. After working so hard to be recognized as a key player this year, I'd blown it by getting all reactionary and emotional.

Even after Rick publicly dumped me, I didn't truly let loose the anger and hurt I felt. I just kept things moving, for fear of how other people would react to my reaction. I didn't want to feed the rumor mill in any way, shape, or form. It made me even more of an expert at burying my feelings. To think, after holding in my emotions so well and for so long, Kelly played a role in my releasing them two times in four days!

I scolded myself. My arms folded across my chest, I silently fumed and watched my team struggle not to lose the second set.

By the time the next set started, Coach Pat had me continue to sit the game out. I didn't blame her. The game was tied right now and I had proven to the team that I was a risk to them today. This just motivated me to work harder next time.

I looked over at Brent again. Now Kelly was talking to him. Rick, meanwhile, was sitting back with a smug look on his face. My heart started racing.

If only life, like school hallways, came equipped with a "break glass in case of emergency" feature. Only a fire drill would save me from what Brent was about to hear. *Think, London, think!* There was nothing I could do from where I was sitting. And to run over there and stop them from meeting would just turn this moment into a bad classic-TV sitcom.

Instead, I mapped out the worst-case scenario. The worst that could happen was Kelly telling Brent that I was just a competition junkie using him for info.

I felt like a sitting duck. It was a good thing Brent seemed to have the patience of a saint. Either that, or he was all about gamesmanship—not letting anyone make him lose his cool. But I didn't have a clue how far Kelly or Rick would take this. They were double-teaming him.

Brent's face suddenly dropped as Kelly and then Rick yammered on and on. "Are you okay, London?" a teammate asked me. I was gnawing on my lower lip and wringing my hands in anxiety. People must have thought I'd straight-up lost my mind today.

"Y-yeah, thanks," I managed to get out.

"It's gonna be okay—everybody has a bad day on the court sooner or later," she said, her voice coated with kindness. It was sweet of her to try to cheer me up. I looked away from the car wreck for a few seconds to give her a smile of thanks.

When I looked back at Brent, he was mouthing off something to Rick, who obviously took offense to what was said. Rick sprang up and grabbed Brent's home-made sign, held it up, and ripped it in two. Intending to rush over to put an end to this, I got out of my seat at the same time Brent did. The guys stood there mean mugging each other, waiting for the other to take the first swing. I got as far as the bottom row of the bleachers before some-one grabbed my arm.

"Where the heck are you going, young lady?" It was Coach Pat wearing a scowl on her face. "Have you lost your mind?" Slowly coming to my senses, I glanced around and saw my teammates on the bench staring at me, waiting for an explanation. When I searched the stands for Brent, he was gone. Only Kelly and Rick stood there looking tickled, like they were at a comedy show. It was clear that the joke was on me.

At the referee's whistle, the game con-tinued on as if nothing had happened. For once I was glad for North Side's loud cheerleaders. They distracted the crowd with some hometown cheer that everyone in the bleachers chanted along with. Coach

Pat benched me for the rest of the game. Mortified, I sat there in miserable silence and watched our team lose.

Aside from Coach Pat's stern earful to me, my teammates didn't bring up my foolishness on the school-bus ride back to Teawood. I guess they could tell that I was distraught enough over everything.

When we got dropped off at school, Rick had the nerve to be there waiting for me. As soon as I stepped off the bus, I marched right to him.

"What do you want?" I demanded to know. "Haven't you done enough damage?"

"Yo, L." He actually looked surprised by my anger. "I just wanted to make sure you had a ride home."

"Oh, c'mon, Rick. Why don't you be honest for once? We both know that what you *really* wanted was to screw me over with Brent."

"It's not even like that," he lied with a straight face. "Anyway, I was hoping that me and you could get back together—"

"What?" I cut him off. "Let's not even go there. First of all, I'm over you. I've moved on and now I really like someone else. And secondly, even if there *was* a chance, do you really think you deserve to get back with someone you cold disrespected? *Uh-uh.* That's not the way things work with me."

Rick had nothing to say. He looked embarrassed, like a child in time-out.

Just then, my dad's car pulled up next to us. *Perfect timing.*

"You really need to check yourself," I told him. There was nothing more to say. I turned around and stepped into the car. Rick stood there and watched us drive away.

Sixteen

I didn't hear from Brent until the next day. After obsessing all night about what it was that he found out, all I got was a short, cryptic text from him: *Tha judges know evrythg. B careful.*

I didn't know exactly what that meant.

"Maybe the judges know that you have a crush on Brent," Pam said during our pow-wow that evening in my room.

"I would die," I wailed, burying my face in my pillow.

"Now who's the one being dramatic here?"

"I know—how did I get this way?"

"First, you're styling better than you thought possible, and now you're believing that the sky is falling. I do believe Trish is right—I'm rubbing off on you."

"How do you think the judges will react to the crush news?" I couldn't think about anything else.

"Well, I don't see how they didn't expect it. The guy's a cutie and he's in the same age group as the contestants. Maybe they'll just slap you on the wrist and call it a day."

I hoped Pam was right. It was bad enough that news about my feelings was probably being broadcast all over Teawood, but for it to be picked up as some behind-the-scenes competition story would be unbearable.

"*Gurl*, need I remind you that you are one of the three finalists?" Pam sprang up from the window seat full of energy. She was done with helping me drag out the pity party. "You just strut your long legs in there on Saturday and keep doing what you've been doing. Represent and be yourself! There are mad people rooting for you."

I pouted and continued finger combing the long tassels on the edge of the pillow in my lap.

"Now let's go lie to your parents about why we need to leave the house at this school-night hour. I have to get there early to help Jake make the party punch."

I nodded.

"You know y'all are crazy, right?"

"Crazy in love like Beyoncé and Jay-Z, *gurl*." She yanked me off my bed.

Week five of the competition was minutes away. My dad drove me to Chic Boutique at 7:45 a.m. on Saturday morning. My mom sat beaming in the passenger seat the whole short ride to the shopping district. "Go get 'em, baby girl," my dad said as I climbed out of the car.

I took a deep breath before walking into the store. My reflection in the glass door showed a determined girl. My hair looked extra funky in the faux-hawk—my new favorite steez. I was rocking my maroon cable-knit sweater dress with the cowl neck. I was getting the hang of wearing a dress more than four times a year. Besides, I'd come to learn that feeling good about how I look is a confidence booster. And I needed all the help I could get today.

The breezy October morning called for a pair of ribbed black tights. I was grateful my kitten-heeled ankle boots were low enough to manage. I couldn't let anyone catch me taking clumsy steps if I was planning to walk out of there with my dignity intact.

All I had to do was make it through the day and then I could go back to my regular life. The last time the judges saw me, they'd watched, puzzled, as I exited the boutique without so much as a "peace out" to them. I had given up, which totally wasn't my style. I couldn't go out like that. No matter how bad things got, I wanted to finish what I'd started. The last thing I had left was my character and I wouldn't let anybody's wicked prank take that away from me.

There was more activity than usual inside the boutique. Lights were set up around the judges' station and there were four chairs instead of three lined up behind it.

Kelly was there already, and so was Pixie. I was usually the early one, so I was sure they were wondering if I'd show up at all.

A superbright light turned on just as I took my usual place next to the leather jacket fixture. I looked over to see Brent adjusting the silver lighting umbrella over the center counter. He seemed focused on his job and oblivious to my presence. He didn't look my way. I didn't want to be caught staring at him so I returned to people watching.

There were folks there that I didn't recognize. A sophisticated woman who wore her tan trench coat like a dress was directing a crew of three people carrying large video cameras on their shoulders.

Lawd, don't let me find out this thing is gonna be televised or something.

A tiny dancer in clown-face makeup must've been krumpin' on my nerve endings because they felt all out of whack. It was one thing to be photographed—you could play off your aversion to spontaneity. But no one could hide in moving pictures. I am horrible at making speeches in front of crowds. As nerdy as it sounds, the only time I don't mind public speaking is in math class. I can go on for days explaining my journey through word problems or algebraic equations. Talking about myself in front of a crowd and in front of cameras is something I can't do.

"Good morning, good morning" rang out Didier's cheerful greeting. It was a relief hearing a familiar voice in all of these surprises. He approached us from behind and walked briskly in the direction of the center counter. The strong aroma of his morning latte wafted to my nose as he rushed by. When he got to his seat, Didier took a slow gulp of his drink before addressing the three of us.

"Welcome, Maya, Kelly, and London, to this final week of the Chic Boutique Model Search." Didier was obviously putting on a show and acting extra formal for the cameras. "We're gonna get started in just a minute." He maintained eye contact with Maya and Kelly but barely looked my way. That awful outsider feeling crept back. "We're just waiting for the lovely Miss Cynthea Bey to join us. She's on her way."

An audible gasp escaped from both Maya and Kelly. As for me, I couldn't have been hit with more of a reason to panic. But instead, I controlled my breathing and reminded myself that I was a top finalist and would behave like one. In just under two hours, it would all be over and I could head home knowing that I didn't let anyone push me out of the competition. No matter how uncomfortable things got, I promised myself that I would not run away from this. I would woman up and end this thing properly. If they asked me to leave, then I would leave. But not a moment before.

"'Ello, girls," Asha said as she joined Didier in her usual chair. Monica followed and sat down at the other end. The seat reserved for Cynthea Bey was between Asha and Monica. Even though it was an exact replica of the others, the chair had a more regal feel to it.

I swallowed hard. Facing Asha's judgmental expressions would be difficult. I prepared myself for her pointy chin and sideways glances. But she didn't look my way.

I wondered if the judges were going to ignore me the entire morning. It was almost as bad as them staring at me in disgust. I didn't know which was worse.

The commotion at the back of the store signaled Cynthea Bey's arrival. One of the photographers took a few snaps of her while she walked up to the store. The model was flanked by two assistants—one of whom had greeted her the day she pulled up to Chic Boutique during casting.

Cynthea looked like a mannequin brought to life. Her attire was much more glam on this day than the last time I'd seen her. She was standing tall in sexy heels with red soles and fishnet stockings. Her skirt was fitted, which showed off her silhouette. She topped off her look with an oversize cashmere shawl that was pinned closed with something blinging. Her hair was worn down, framing her famous face with a cascade of layered bone-straight strands. It was amazing how different she looked today.

All of this fanfare underscored how big this day was to Face, Chic Boutique, and Cynthea Bey. It reminded me how unlikely it was that I'd made it this far. It also made me want to beg the judges to rid me of my duties as a token contestant. This was too big a deal for me to be a part of. What did I know about modeling and looking fabulous? I never had the urge to stand in front of a wind machine. I was suddenly sorry that I signed up for the competition. I was sorry things had drawn out this far.

After breaking from the gaggle of people who crowded Cynthea with questions and updates, the megawatt star finally made her way to her seat behind the counter.

"Good morning, Maya," she said, pausing to acknowledge the contestant in first place. "Good morning, Kelly," she continued, holding eye contact with the second-place contestant. "Good morning, London." Her voice was just as welcoming as it had been for the other two girls. She warmly smiled at me, and the smile reached her eyes.

I swallowed hard—twice. Just hearing her say my name was a jolt. I didn't know whether to laugh or cry.

The woman in the trench coat dress silently directed one of the three swarming camera crew members to take two steps closer to Cynthea for a better angle.

"I want to congratulate the three of you for making it to the final week of the competition." Cynthea sat poised as she spoke. "I have been following everything closely and I am proud of the selections that *Face Magazine*'s readers have made. From this point on, though, the final choices will be ours."

Asha finally pointed her chin in my direction. Her eyes darted from my boots up to my faux-hawk, then back down again. That was all I got before she went back to staring at Kelly and Maya. I shifted my weight from one foot to another. That tiny kitten heel was started to feel like a pebble underneath my foot.

"For this final challenge, we've invited a production team to come down to film your answers to the questions we will be asking you. We've seen what you can do, but today we'd like to *hear* directly from you. The chosen Chic Boutique model will be going on interviews and will be shooting online commercials, so we'd like to hear as well as see how you present yourself to the world."

This is the final nail in my coffin, I thought. Oh, where was that emergency glass when you needed it?

"First up, Maya." Cynthea's smile faded and she focused her attention on Pixie. "Please step forward."

Trench Coat Lady directed Maya to the strips of masking tape that marked an X in front of the counter. I could see the supermodel in Maya creeping out as she walked up to it.

Seventeen

Pixie stood with both feet directly over the X. After a few seconds, she shifted her weight to one leg as she waited for Cynthea's probing question.

"Maya Kwon," Cynthea started, her torso leaning closer to the counter, "why do you think you should win this competition?"

Pixie looked down for a second, her hair falling to the front of her face. I'd seen her do this before when she wanted to gather her thoughts or prepare herself for something challenging. I wondered if when she did this, she paused time and astrally projected to some alternate universe where she was issued the right answer to say. Maybe while she was in that other universe, we were all frozen and would be none the wiser when she returned. Perhaps it was also during this time that Pixie threw on her Sasha Fierce costume—which, however powerful, was invisible to everyone else.

When she lifted her face, Pixie did indeed look more confident and ready to fire out a response.

"I think I should win this competition," she began like a fifth grader trained to give the teacher full answers, "because to me, fashion isn't about status, fads, or name brands. It's about art, expression, and culture." *Nice start*, I thought, but continued holding my breath for her.

"I'm someone who understands that clothes can make statements about our personalities, our moods, and our personal style. I love how Chic Boutique gives young people access not only to the latest trends but to the tools of self-expression. It would be an honor to represent Chic Boutique and be a part of the team that offers young women more options in self-expression. I enjoy interpreting the styles that the boutique has to offer and I know that my modeling will bring new meaning to clothes and more imagination to young people."

There was a pause of silence after she'd spoken. Cynthea Bey and the judges reacted by adjusting themselves in their seats as if the spell they'd been under, which had transfixed them, had been broken when Pixie stopped speaking.

"Thank you, Maya." Cynthea was visibly impressed. "That was lovely to hear." She nodded a few times. "The judges and I want to congratulate you on a job well done these past few weeks. You've demonstrated your natural talent for modeling and you have a lovely personality to go along with that. So, thank you. It was a pleasure to have you in this competition."

The judges echoed their thank-yous and Didier raised his coffee cup to salute Pixie.

I exhaled—for now.

"Next, Kelly Fletcher, please step forward." Cynthea laid one hand over the other on the counter and waited for Pixie to relinquish the X spot to Kelly.

Kelly clickety-clacked her way over like a VIP cutting the line outside the X Spot club. Her paces seemed deliberate and choreographed.

I hated to admit that she looked more gorgeous than usual. Her open-sleeved belted dress had a straight-off-the-runway look to it. I didn't recognize it as having come from Chic Boutique. I'd almost memorized every rack during last week's challenge. Kelly's makeup accented her almond-shaped eyes, and her lips were a perfect shade of burgundy. She folded her manicured hands in front of her and leaned on one hip as she placed her feet on either side of the X.

"Kelly," Cynthea started once Kelly was settled, "why do you think you deserve to win this competition?"

Kelly answered right away, but in a voice I didn't recognize. Her tone was softer than normal and at a slightly higher pitch. It was her way of trying to sound as innocent as possible.

"I think I deserve to win this competition because I have been working my entire life for this moment. I started modeling as a child, and I enjoyed the thrill of showing up on set and seeing the cameras set up, ready to capture my moments in front of them. It amazed me how easily I warmed up to the lens and how much fun it was. But all those times, I didn't have a choice whether or not to show up to the castings. My family put me into the modeling business even before

I was able to speak up for myself. And now that I'm older and I've had a chance to think about it, I discovered that I do love modeling. I was the one who took that step. No one forced me into it this time. It was my choice and I chose to pursue modeling. And what better way to break back into it than through a modeling icon like you, Cynthea Bey, a professional I have admired for so long."

Instead of silence following Kelly's statement, exhales puffed out of the judges. It was as if they had all been holding their breath, hoping that she said all the right things. And in their opinion, she had.

Kelly's response echoed in my mind. Hearing her story caused a ripple of understanding to flow through me. It made me realize that as an only child, she never fully had the freedom to do what she wanted. By comparison, my childhood was more freestyle—thanks to the hecticness of having twin brothers. There was no pressure to perform at an intense level. Even though I complained that my parents weren't enthusiastic about my volleyball, I cringed when imagining them being overly obsessed with my stats and my game performances.

"Thank you, Kelly." Cynthea offered the sincere comfort of her words. "And I too want to congratulate you on the fantastic presence in this competition. I can see why your family pushed you into modeling. You were made for it. And even if you change your mind and decide not to pursue a modeling career in the future, we are all confident that wherever you go, you will bring your inspiring brand of style to the people you come in contact with. We are truly proud of the professionalism you brought to every challenge—even when things didn't go as smoothly as expected." I gulped in shame at the reference to my outburst. "You have truly shown grace under pressure, and for that we thank you."

Whatever Cynthea said next was muffled by the sound of my heart pounding in my ears. I was next to the X. As soon as Cynthea's lips stopped moving, Kelly vacated the spot as confidently as she had approached it.

Suddenly, I felt the heat of the judges' focus on me.

"London Abrams," Cynthea began like clockwork, "please step forward."

Thanks to my athletic team training, my

body responded to the request and directed my size nines to the X. No one picked up on the fact that I was trembling. I kept my feet together and my hands linked behind my back. I mentally went over the answer I thought would work best for tonight's question and prepared myself to deliver it.

"London," the supermodel began, "what was your *real* reason for signing up for this competition?"

Eighteen

I was cold busted.

My mouth was so dry, my tongue stuck to the roof. I had to shake off the stunned look on my face quickly, before it got picked up by the cameras. Just the thought of how humiliated my parents would be if my reaction became a YouTube classic was sobering enough.

I swallowed down the lump of fear that was lodged in my throat. Cynthea and the judges expected a prompt reply and I was going to give them one.

My lips parted, but no dazzling explanation jumped out and performed a tap dance for them. There was no wannabe London left in there to come out. The jig was up, and the truth was all I had left.

"I signed up for the competition because I was hoping to use my filled-out application as a conversation piece. I wanted to get to know a certain someone better and I thought this was my only chance at doing it. Auditioning was something so far from my intentions." The words flowed out of me. Telling the truth was easier once you got going. I continued, "And honestly, from the look of the superpretty girls on the casting line, I didn't think I stood the slightest chance of even getting considered as a contestant. I mean, I'm not nearly as striking. It's an accepted fact that I'm just not model material. But I was shocked when I got the call telling me that I was selected. I even thought the call was a prank!"

In an effort to control the wells of tears I felt flooding my eyes, I cleared my throat and paused to shift my weight to the other leg. Blinking right at this moment would send tears streaming, so I looked at the beams along the vaulted ceiling.

"All along, I was the only person truly counting myself out. The judges saw something in me that I didn't." My voice cracked. "And because of the amazing photography, the readers picked up on that same thing. Modeling for this competition didn't call for anything but for me to be myself, and for that I'm grateful. I learned to have fun with different expressions of myself. So, no, I didn't sign up because I had any deep-seated aspirations to be a model. But in the end, I have become a model. A model who not only represents the clothes but the girls who wear them. It was my pleasure doing this. I never thought of myself as a representative, but I'm proud to have been considered one."

I used the judges' reflective silence to wipe the tear that was tumbling down my cheek. How humiliating it was to be outed as a phony. Now all of cyberworld would know that I was boy crazy enough to join a competition I had no business being in.

There was nothing I could do to control the jaw-jacking that I was sure would follow.

I thought of Brent. He was nowhere on the set, but all I could think of was avoiding him for the rest of my time in Teawood or in New Jersey in general. I'd caused him enough trouble. The amount of wackiness that I had shown that boy was enough of an embarrassment to ensure that this was the last time I would plan on seeing him.

"Thank you, London." Cynthea had regained her composure. While I was explaining my sordid tale, she blinked so many times, I was worried her false eyelashes would pop off. I didn't get a look at the other judges, but from the quality of the silence coming from them, I could tell they too were taken aback.

"Your honesty was as refreshing as it was brave. For that you have my respect. And after talking things over with the judges, we were all impressed with the maturity in which you recovered in this competition. It's not easy feeling like the underdog. But we agree that your place in this competition was an important one. You bring a unique face to the competition and your modeling skills jump out in a photograph. We were happy to have you participate."

My maturity? I thought I acted like a complete brat. A total sore loser. It was validating to hear that the judges did take note of my apology and were willing to put it behind them. Not too many people would get such a second chance. I was humbled to hear this.

Cynthea's nod indicated that I should return to my position next to the leather jacket rounder.

"Well." Cynthea looked like she was as winded as we all were after those tense moments. Slowly, the air was getting more relaxed. The questions were over and the rest was up to the judges. "This concludes our very first Chic Boutique Model Search. I was proud of the contestants chosen, and now comes the hard part in deciding who will be chosen for our spring ad campaign. That answer will not come today."

With that statement, Kelly, Pixie, and I all went from attention to at ease.

"Thank you for coming. Please report back here at the same time tomorrow for our official announcement. Don't worry— we won't keep you long. We know you'll want the extra time to get ready for tomorrow night's Face of Spring Gala." The modeling search closing soiree was to take place the following evening, and workers had already constructed a stage for the event. Lots of boldfaced names from the industry would be in attendance and local press would be covering the grand event. All fifteen contestants were invited back to join the party.

At that moment, I couldn't get out of Chic Boutique fast enough. As I was exiting the store, Kelly caught up to me.

"Hey, London," she called out to me in the friendliest tone. The fakery was a show for the video camera crew, because her voice changed once we were outside the glass doors. "Can you hook me up with one of Brent's inside tips to help me prepare for tomorrow? Oh, that's right—he asked you not to tell me." Before I could react, she strutted to the parked SUV waiting for her at the curb.

She knows that Brent told me about the cash prize. Or was she just playing mind games?

I walked home an alternate way in case anyone else wanted to catch up with me. I was in no mood for talking—I had done too much of that already. I don't know if I was half-expecting the camera crew to follow me like I was on some reality TV show. I would've been the perfect train-wreck character to glue eyes to the tube. I wasn't going to allow myself to be anyone's sideshow anymore.

"Hey, baby girl," my dad called out when he saw me rounding the front walkway of our house. I'd dragged my feet all the way home, so by the time I got there, I had amassed a following of multicolored leaves around my feet. It was damn near ankle-deep but I didn't care. Dad was stuffing a large gym bag in the trunk of his car. "I thought you were gonna text me when you were ready."

Not having the wherewithal to verbally answer, I tipped my head to one side and shrugged in response.

The minute he saw the look on my face, Dad walked over to me before I could reach for the front door.

"Hey, hey," he said soothingly as he wrapped me up in a bear hug. I buried my face in his chest and the tears flowed. "Just remember, you shook things up by joining this competition. That's an admirable thing to do in a world where people stick to what's safe. And that's something you should never regret or be ashamed of. I'm proud of you."

I didn't want to break out the ugly cry in front of my house, so I nodded my thanks, then broke away and headed indoors. Before I could reach for the doorknob, Warren and Wyatt swung open the door and rushed out like two escapees.

"What's wrong with London?" I heard them ask my dad.

"Give your sister some space," he warned them. "And c'mon—you know your capoeira class starts in five minutes. Whatchy'all been doing in there?"

Their weak excuses were cut off when the door slammed shut.

"Boys, if y'all don't stop slamming that door—!" My mom rushed out from the kitchen ready to ream the twins for banging up the house. She always joked about how the house had started aging in dog years once the twins learned how to walk.

"Sweetie," she breathed out when she saw the zombielike way I was walking up the stairs. "What's wrong? How did things go today?"

"I don't really wanna talk about it right now." I stopped midstep. She looked at the sadness drooping my eyes and she backed off.

"Okay, honey." She walked closer to me. "Can I get you anything?"

My mom's soothing voice was like a

switch that turned on the tear production all over again.

"No." I hiccupped. "I just want to be alone."

"Okay." She respected my wishes.

When I reached my bedroom, I grabbed my favorite pillow and clutched it like it was my last lifesaver in a sea of doubt.

Five weeks had passed since the start of the competition, and I was not as close to Brent or my volleyball tuition as I had planned to be. My dad talked about not regretting my decisions, but with results like these, I couldn't help wondering what I'd really gotten out of it.

Brent probably thought I was the biggest head case he'd ever come across. I'd put his job in jeopardy by showing up and being obvious about my feelings for him. I had lost him for sure. To think, I actually was attracted to him and giddy around him. I daydreamed about him whenever I wasn't with him.

But now reality was setting in pretty fast and it was time for me to face the facts. Brent and I couldn't be together. I couldn't bear to see him because it would only remind me of the crazy encounters and off-the-wall behavior that I'd exhibited these past few weeks. What's more, I was short five hundred dollars for the summer camp registration fee and there was no way I would earn that money in the two weeks I had left. And with the way my luck was going, I doubt I stood a chance to win that contest cash prize. Besides, that money felt kind of tainted now that the word may be out that Brent told me about it.

Because of a crazy whim I'd ruined my chances to go to camp. It was something I'd been dreaming about for so long, but I would have to wait another year to get it. That was a tough blow for me to take. Fresh tears streamed down my face.

Why did I have to screw things up in such a major way? I thought about my parents never straying from their game plan. Had I taken a page from their book, none of this would have ever happened. I would've been on track to pay for the volleyball camp fee. But also in that alternate universe, I would not have come to know Brent. And I wouldn't have realized the things I now know—that I could model and that supporters wished me the best with it.

A knock on the door snapped me from that alternate universe.

"London." It was my mother. "How are you feeling?"

My back was to the door and I lay clutching my pillow. My shoes were on. I was all dressed up but feeling like crap. A few seconds later, I felt her sit down next to me and rest her hand on my back.

"Honey, I've been thinking about what you must've been going through these past few weeks," she began softly. "And I have to apologize for not considering your feelings so much as pushing for my silly dream to see your face in print."

I blinked a few tears out of my flooded eyes but remained silent.

"It was unfair for me to do that to you, and I'm sorry. When I saw that Kelly Fletcher was in the competition, something totally silly in me just kicked into gear. That is not the type of mother I want to be. And it made me realize that this wasn't the first time that I'd done this to you. When I think of all the drama I put you through with those castings and competitive ridiculousness with Mrs. Fletcher . . . honey, I'm so sorry."

My tears dried up as I listened to my

mother's words. I hadn't even realized that she was aware of how she'd carried on back then. But more surprising, I was surprised to feel how much of a relief her words were to hear. A tenseness I hadn't even known existed in my chest suddenly softened. I felt like I had just sat in front of the Vicks humidifier that Mom used to put on in the boys' room to clear up their congestion. I breathed easily. That was enough to make me wipe the tears from the corners of my eyes and exhale.

When I sat up, Mom was there with a warm hug. As I finally pulled away from her, she cupped my face in her hands.

"You are gorgeous just the way you are, and you don't have to audition for or win any modeling contest for me to see that."

That made me smile. She continued scanning my face and then asked, "Have you been using that acne cream I gave you?" She cupped my chin, angling my head closer to the light coming in from the window. "You must be doing something out of order because you're not reaching this area right here—"

I moved my head from her clutches and backed away to the corner of the bed. "No, Mother." I shook my head. "And thank you for ruining our little moment."

"Nobody's gonna tell you the truth like your momma can." She stood up, her playfulness back in full swing the way I like it. "I do it because I *luuv* ya."

"Lucky me," I told her, pretending to be overly excited.

"Now, come down and have something to eat. You must be starving."

Santogold's "The Creator" rang out, but I couldn't figure out where my phone was.

"I'll be down in a minute," I told her before she closed the door behind her.

I lifted my Olympics pillow and then dug through a few others until I found it.

"Pam, hey," I answered before it went to voice mail.

"Gurrrrl," she started, "I know you must have crazy stuff to tell me about your morning at Chic Boutique. I already know they're holding off on choosing the winner until tomorrow, so I'll go first and tell you what I gotta tell you."

Pam didn't take a breath and I didn't stop her.

"Check out what your loverboy Brent posted on Flickr. Do not pass Go and check it out now."

I was already firing up my laptop.

"Okay, give me a few seconds," I said to slow her down.

"I always knew that guy was the truth. London, he's nothing like the triflin' likes of Rick. I really like him for you. I've never seen you this excited about a guy ever."

There was a photo of me in the juice bar from the day that Brent and I had our first kiss. He even wrote something to go along with the photo: *Introducing the baddest chick on the volleyball court. She's nasty against the net and has the sweetest personality to match her sweet spiking skills. Watch out.*

"Hello?" I heard Pam call out on the other end. "Are you there?"

"I . . . yeah." I kept rereading Brent's description of me posted just that morning—hours before my Chic Boutique confession. "I'm just surprised that he feels that way and is open enough to blast it on Flickr!"

Outside my door, I heard my front doorbell ring. If it was one of my mother's friends, I would stay inside my room for a little longer. I didn't feel like playing host to anyone right now.

"Believe it, London," Pam was saying. "I think it's so cool that he's not caring how it looks and he went for it anyway."

At that moment, my mom softly knocked on my door.

"London," she whispered when she poked her head in. "There's a young man downstairs to see you. He says his name is Brent."

Nineteen

"Pam, I gotta go." I kept my eye on the door on the spot where my mom had just been. "Brent is downstairs waiting to see me."

"Aaaah!" Pam almost injured my eardrum. "Go, go, go! And call me back *as soon* as he leaves."

I hung up, then rushed over to my mirror. My eyes looked a little bit bloodshot from all the crying I had done. I rummaged through my drawer and found my tiny emergency bottle of Visine. After squeezing one drop in each eye, I blinked a few times and straightened up my clothes and smoothed down my hair. I kicked off my shoes and threw on a pair of comfy black flats. My lip color had faded, but the clear lip gloss I threw on worked just fine.

I didn't know what to expect, but when I went down to the living room, Brent was sitting on the bench in front of the piano. He stood up as soon as he saw me.

"Hi, London." He stuffed his hands in his pockets and took a few paces toward me. I recognized that bashful-licious stance from the first day we met.

"I hope you don't mind me stopping by. You left before I had the chance to give you this." Brent went back to the bench and picked up the slim, large object leaning against it. "This is for you, London," he said, handing it to me. It was a frame and it was heavier than he'd made it seem.

I held it with both hands but didn't remove the white tissue paper from around it. My mind was reeling. First I thought about how great it was to see him—here, standing in front of me and in my home. Next the fact that he'd brought something for me was even more touching.

"Aren't you gonna look at it?" he asked me.

"Oh, yeah." I chuckled. Brent reached out and helped me take off the paper.

It was a black wooden-framed picture of me on the court from the day Brent came to shadow me. I was holding up my hand with the number one sign in the air. The proud look on my face said it all—I felt good about myself and it showed. Seeing how happy I looked made me smile. I remembered the exact moment when that shot was taken. I was looking up to the stands at Pam, right after she called my name.

"This is amazing." My voice was quiet because I was so humbled by his gesture. "Thank you so much."

I didn't look up from the frame. The look in my eyes would've definitely given me away, and I wanted to play it cool. It was bad enough that he knew that I'd signed up for the competition just to meet him. What if he also thought I had followed him to work from Art Attack? The risk of acting like a total stalker was too high. If I looked up, he would've read in my eyes that I was head over heels and wanted to stick a GPS chip on his sneaker laces so we could always cross paths.

Okay, maybe that was a bit much. But if you stripped down the Pamisms, the point was that I didn't want him to know that

I liked him a lot. I'd embarrassed myself enough as it was.

"London, I don't know if this is worth anything, but I'm sorry for the way things went down." Brent sounded like he was confessing something he wasn't proud of. "When Kelly and Rick talked to me that day at your game, I didn't know what to think. I should've reached out to you to hear your side of the story, but at the time, I felt played in a way. A few days before, when you and Kelly had it out, I spoke up for you. I told Didier that things might not have gone down as they seemed to. And then when Kelly insinuated that you told her about the cash prize, I felt played for having risked my job to defend you."

I hadn't realized that he'd done that. Only a good friend would stick their neck out for someone like that. The complete opposite of what a foe would do. A foe with a faux personality, like Kelly. I felt my lips tighten in growing anger at the thought of Kelly lying about me to Brent. *She insinuated that I told him about the cash prize?* My heart rate quickened. But in the next breath, I caught myself. I was playing right into that tit-for-tat cycle from hell—Kelly pushes my button, I get heated and then push back. And when the smoke clears, the only straight-thinking person left standing is Brent, defending me to his boss.

"Wow," I finally said. "You told Didier that?"

Brent smirked and nodded. "I know—stupid, huh?"

"More like sweet." I nodded. "I'm the one who should be apologizing to you. The way I exposed you to the ridiculousness between me and Kelly was wrong. I'm sorry for sticking you in the middle of Kelly, Rick, and this whole mess."

"But I created this mess by telling you about the prize. I told Didier what I'd done, and understandably, he terminated my internship."

My eyes welled up with tears and I covered my mouth in shock. I felt horrible.

Brent put his hand on my shoulder and gently squeezed.

"It's okay. This is how it had to go down. I wouldn't feel right if they'd ask me to stay. Besides, sports photography is opening up some doors for me. That's the direction I want to be heading in anyway."

I nodded and swallowed hard.

"Are you okay?" he asked. "Still in shock?"

"No, I'm just surprised he didn't sic Asha on you. That woman's chin is a deadly weapon."

We both cracked up. It felt good to laugh it off.

"But don't sleep on Asha—she had your back too," Brent said.

"That's something I find very hard to believe," I told him. She was the last person I believed had any interest in me. "Asha was the one who always had this air of disappointment when she looked at me." I shook my head, doubting that he'd read the judgmental judge right.

"Well, that may be, but homegirl was the only one who agreed with me. She said that you didn't seem like the type to break out like a diva for no reason."

This was definitely the flip side of how I thought things would go today.

"I feel horrible about the way I behaved every time Kelly baited me. I don't know why anyone would bother to have my back after the way that I acted."

"It's because they also know that you are a sweet, funny person with a lot of heart on and off the court. And like me, they admire your natural beauty." Brent locked his eyes with mine. I was mesmerized by them. The dimple on the right side of his face deepened as he smirked again. He was probably laughing at how lost I was getting in his eyes. I blinked and looked back at the photo.

"You know, in a couple of years, a photo by Brent St. John is gonna go for a brick on eBay," I said in an effort to change the subject.

"No, you mean a photo of gold medalist London Abrams is gonna be valuable."

"Just don't forget to tell everyone where you got your start in sports photography, n'kay?"

"Look for me—I'll be the one getting knocked over by Lebron James when he chases a ball off the court."

"Those poor bastards—I always feel bad when that happens."

Even though we were joking, Brent seemed concerned about the sad and slightly bloodshot look in my eyes.

"How are we gonna cheer each other up?" he asked.

My eyebrows perked up. "I've got an idea, but you gotta leave behind your camera for one evening."

"I'm listening," Brent responded cautiously.

"Will you be my date for tomorrow's Face of Spring Gala?"

"If I can get past the bouncers on the lookout for ex-interns, *yes*."

We busted out laughing again. In the next moment, Brent reached out and pulled me in for a warm hug. It felt nice being in his arms. After a few moments, we didn't step away from each other. Instead, Brent looked down and found my lips with his. It was a picture-perfect kiss.

Later that day, I met Pam at her house so that we could check out Facemag.com together. After a trying, drama-filled day of emotional roller coasters, I couldn't bear getting into something else—at least, not alone. Plus, her house was the most private place (meaning a Warren-and-Wyatt-free zone) for us to assess the damage.

"Okay, here goes." Pam prepared me before clicking around on her screen. I was on her king-size bed, hugging my legs and resting my chin on my knees while watching Pam at her desk.

"The video posts are up of the Q and A,"

she announced. "Are you sure you want to see it? Because you don't have to watch it if you don't want to. If you think it'll just make you feel worse, then don't bother."

I stopped gnawing on my lower lip to say, "No, I want to know just what I'm dealing with so that I'll be ready for whatever people throw my way. Start it."

Pam didn't click the play button at first. She waited until she was convinced by the look in my eyes.

I pulled up a chair next to her and for the next ten minutes, we watched in silence. The video was edited to include reaction shots from the judges that I hadn't seen. Everyone looked slightly different on film. For one, all of our heads looked so much bigger.

When it was my turn in the hot spot, I cringed when I saw just how many twitches and weird facial expressions I make when talking.

"Stop—you look fine, London," Pam scolded me when I winced and backed away from my face on the screen.

It was all there for anyone who visited the site to see. Me in my teary confession. My effort to control the tears by looking at the ceiling was a smart decision. It didn't look as bad as I thought it would. No runny nose or awkward hiccups. That happened later, after I got home.

"Wow," Pam whispered. When I looked at her, her eyes were a bit glassy.

"You okay?" I asked her.

"That was a bold thing to do, London," she said. "I admire that about you. It shows that you have integrity."

"Gurl, if she had given me the same question she asked everyone else, I wouldn't have even went there," I admitted. "But you know what? I'm glad she did."

The next morning, the judges were prepared to announce their choice for the Chic Boutique model for the upcoming spring season. The scene in the store was more low-key. Just the judges and two photographers were there with Cynthea Bey.

The famous supermodel was early for this meeting and didn't waste any time getting down to business. Kelly and Pixie were dressed down in jeans, as was I. It felt great to be able to relax in my favorite pair of American Eagle jeans and, yes, my volleyball jersey. At that point, I figured I had nothing else to lose.

"Ladies, this is the moment we've all been waiting for," Cynthea started. Even she was rocking some laid-back fuzzy boots and tights with a minidress. "And I have to say, it was a tough decision to make, so the judges and I took an unconventional approach."

Kelly, Pixie, and I weren't holding hands and hugging one another while awaiting the decision like they do in the Miss America pageant. But somehow, I felt like we were more on the same wavelength than we'd been during the entire contest. We shot glances at one another as if to wish one another good luck. Pixie and I went so far as to nod kindly to each other. Something had changed between the day before and now. The pressure to measure up was gone. The dust had cleared for the most part, and we were left with some unlikely bond for having been through it together.

"Modeling is something you have to have passion for. It's a tough business to be in and it takes a certain type of person to make it. And the modeling contract with Bey Agency is one that is an opportunity of a lifetime, so we wanted to give it to a person with heart for the game. For this Face of

Spring honor, our girl had to possess a sense of fun, freedom, and adventure. Of course, this person had to have a nice build to model the clothes. But we were also interested in a Jersey girl with local sensibilities. Before we started our search, we thought this was an ambitious list of criteria that would be tough to find in one person. But after carefully considering both her performance during the challenges and the way in which she was received by Facemag.com readers, we're confident that we've found everything and more in this contestant."

Pixie started fidgeting where she stood. Kelly held her head higher as if bracing for a recovery in the event that she was passed over. It was like that look Oscar nominees have just after they lose to someone else. I didn't bat an eye. I knew exactly who the more model-minded two-thirds of us were. Anything less would have been totally unfair.

"On this day we are so proud to accept Maya Kwon into the Bey Agency. And congratulations, Maya, on being crowned Chic Boutique's Face of Spring."

Maya screamed in utter delight. It was the loudest sound to come out of her during this entire competition. She seemed thrown by the honor. Tears streamed down her face as she screamed a second time. The judges stood up and applauded Maya.

This was when the pageant element came into play. Kelly walked to Pixie with her arms outstretched. I was surprised to see that much emotion come spilling out of Kelly like it had been bottled just below the surface for a long time.

She wasn't a robot after all.

I hugged Maya next.

"Congratulations," I told her. "I'm so happy for you."

As cliché as that sounded, it was the truth. Kelly and I didn't exchange any pleasantries. I didn't have a thing to say to her. But I had the feeling she was coming to the same conclusion as me—we'd defeated ourselves by reviving our pointless childhood competition.

Twenty

When my family and I turned down Chic Boutique's street, we could see that there was fanfare outside the store. Traffic had slowed because of the valet parking the boutique had set up just for the night.

"Woo-wee," my dad said, echoing his own father's favorite reaction. "I see you have friends in high places, London. La-ti-*da*."

"That's only because she's so dang tall." Wyatt couldn't resist taking a shot.

Warren looked at him like he was crazy. I never understood how they could be so night-and-day.

"Said the chump sittin' on the hump," I shot back from my window seat next to him.

Everyone in the car chuckled

"We're next on the valet line." My mom pulled down her passenger-seat visor and popped open the mirror on it. She finger combed her short curly hair and rubbed her lips together to smooth over her bronze lipstick. She looked amazing. Dad couldn't stop saying "Woo-wee" as we were leaving the house. Even my father and the twins looked sharp with their dapper suits on. Dad was a firm believer in straying from the clinical white shirts, so he and the boys all rocked striped or pastel-colored shirts and ties to go with their dark suits.

Monica the judge was too happy to go over wardrobe selections with me for the evening. It was complements of Chic Boutique. A rack of evening gowns was delivered to the boutique earlier in the day and was waiting for me in the basement. I was invited down to try on a few. Monica was superhelpful in pinpointing the right dress for my body and my personal taste. We both agreed that the maroon off-the-shoulder cocktail dress was the best choice.

Layla came over to help me style my hair. We let it down in all its curly fro glory. It was a look I only ever rock at home. But with some Carol's Daughter styling products and lots of hair pins, she was able to pull it off so it didn't look too puffy. I loved it. Next, she'd hooked up my makeup with a barely there touch of glimmering eye shadow and pink-glazed gloss on my lips. It was all I was willing to put on. I still wanted to recognize myself at the end of the day.

"Remember, boys," Mom said as she put the visor back up and turned to face us in the backseat, "don't embarrass yourselves in there tonight. Because you sure ain't gonna embarrass us."

As we pulled up, I spotted Brent waiting for me on the sidewalk. He looked so dreamy all dressed up in a black wool coat and a smile. My family got out of the car and stepped right onto the red carpet leading to the front door of the boutique. The valet drove our family car to an offsite parking area.

"Oh, hello, young man." My mother recognized Brent, who was waiting to walk in with me.

"Hello, Mrs. Abrams," he responded politely. His former intern partner started snapping away at us.

"You look beautiful, London," he said, watching me from the side.

My cheeks got warm despite the evening temperature.

"Awww." Wyatt seized the opportunity. He started to say something but decided against it when he caught my mother's glare.

"Can I get you all standing close together?" the other photographer called out. When we huddled, he snapped two or three flashbulbs in our faces.

"We also need a shot of London by herself." He instructed me to stand in the center of the red carpet.

"Take off your coat!" Mom called out after he snapped a few. I looked at her like she was crazy.

"It'll only be for a few seconds." She was already next to me, tugging the coat off. "The stars do it all the time. You'll be happy that you did it when you see my pictures."

I shot a look at my dad so that he would come get his woman. He looked away and whistled.

"Come on, boys, let's get inside," he finally said with a smirk. "It's freezing out here!"

The twins chimed in with wicked laughs

and followed Dad through the double glass doors.

"Oh, it's like that, huh?" I called after them.

Mom pulled away with my coat and my bare arms tingled like, *What are we doing exposed like this?* I held my clutch purse in front of me with both hands, shifted my weight to one leg, and posed for three quick shots.

Mom was back with my coat in no time.

"So folks don't think I'm mistreating my child," she said while helping me get it back on. As soon as we walked in, we found my dad and brothers picking hors d'oeuvres off a waiter's platter.

Chic Boutique was decked out. There were velvet curtains draping across the ceiling beams. The chandelier lights were dimmed, creating a ballroom feel in the warehouse space. Racks of clothes were neatly tucked to the sides, and a gigantic area rug was laid down. Jazz music was playing on the speaker system, instead of the usual sounds of hip-hop or rock. A black makeshift platform was erected where the center counter usually was. Three microphones stood on the platform, which was flanked by more velvet curtains.

"Congratulations, London." Mrs. Fletcher cut off our intended path. She briefly turned her attention to Mom. "Hello, Lydia. Long time."

"Yes, it has been." I could tell Mom was wondering what in the hell Mrs. Fletcher did to her face. It looked like she'd timed her Botox injections too close to tonight's event. The woman's face was as tight as Mariah Carey's outfit.

Although she said it pleasantly, Mom didn't stick around to make any small talk with Mrs. Fletcher.

Dad and the boys chewed their way around the room as they followed us through the store. I introduced my parents to Pixie and Asha.

Next, Brent and I broke away from the clan to talk to Pam for a few minutes. The girl was making the most of her honorary press pass to the event. She was busy interviewing people about what they had on. This was more access to the fashion-obsessed than Pam had ever run into in Teawood. She was like a kid in a candy store, snapping digital shots of people and jotting down details of their fashion story. Pam wasn't interested in hearing people drone on about labels and designers' names. She was curious about the personal touches they'd added to their look—the vintage pin, the crocheted appliqué on their gloves, their choice of dress color, the way they styled their hair. I couldn't wait to read her blog the next day.

"Your *gurl* Asha introduced herself to me a few minutes ago," Pam told me breathlessly when she found me by the pasta station. "She read my blog and wants to feature me on Facemag.com!"

"Are you serious? That's dope!" I was excited for her.

"Well, not feature me. It's more of a few short sentences for a short sidebar about American teens who blog called 'Local Blogs by Local Girls.' Anyway, there's gonna be a map of the U.S., and if you click New Jersey, I'll be included in their top five blogs to visit for this state."

"Hotness." I was so proud of her.

"Gotta go." Pam eyed someone rocking an Afro-punk look and approached them with her pen and pad in hand.

Finally, Brent and I were alone again.

"Notice something?" I asked him.

"You mean that you're by far the prettiest

princess at the ball?" He touched my arm.

I lowered my eyelids and smiled to keep from gushing. "No, silly," I told him playfully. "What I meant is that you got past the castle guards without being discovered as a foe of this kingdom."

"They saw me," he said confidently. "But they figured they can't beat me." Brent pretended to straighten the tie of his very-retro-Motown-recording-artist suit. He looked so fine. I was staring so hard, I didn't notice Monica walk up beside me.

"London." She tapped me on the shoulder. "We're going to get started. We need you on stage."

Just then my dad came over and started drilling Brent about his family background. I winced at Brent apologetically as I excused myself and followed Monica.

"Ladies and gentlemen." A radiant Cynthea Bey called everyone's attention to the makeshift stage. The crowd quieted down and the jazz music was lowered. "Thank you for joining us here tonight."

Kelly, Maya, and I stood offstage. We were asked to wait for our names to be called. I got nervous about the idea of going up the stage steps in heels. I barely heard a word Cynthea was saying, but the crowd interrupted her with applause now and then. When she called the judges to the stage, I watched Didier, Monica, and Asha climb up and say a few words.

Next, Maya was invited onstage. I clapped as she gracefully stepped up and walked across the platform to accept the Bey Modeling Agency certificate. She paused for photos next to the contest judges and then they stepped aside. As Maya turned to step off the stage, Cynthea held on to Maya's hand.

"Not so fast. We have a special surprise for you. Along with your certificate, we are happy to give you this check for fifteen hundred dollars."

The audience cheered again, and Maya walked away blushing with giddiness. I clapped and let out a *woot*, pleased that Pixie had gotten the cash prize.

"At this time we'd like give an honorable mention to our two talented runners-up, London Abrams and Kelly Fletcher," Cynthea shouted into the mic.

I studied the platform steps to prepare for my climb. Tripping up there would be a disaster. I looked at the crowd and spotted my dad's head above everyone else's. He was taking a picture of me with his digital camera. He put a thumbs-up sign in the air and I smiled.

The crowd cheered and camera flashes went off. I carefully stepped onstage, and I had a bounce in my step as I walked over to Cynthea's waiting arms. She went back on the mic when the cheers died down.

"London and Kelly, as thanks for being a part of this exciting competition, Chic Boutique and Bey Productions are proud to award you each with a check for one thousand dollars."

The crowd erupted again. A check for *one thousand dollars?* This was so unexpected. The only thing swirling in my mind at that moment was *Peak Performance Summer Volleyball Camp!* I had to fight back the tears of gratitude.

"We thank all of you contestants for being in this competition. I'm sure I speak on behalf of the judges when I say that it was a pleasure to meet all of you."

After the presentations, everyone got off the stage. We were led over to the photo set near the back corner of the store. We took group pictures of the fifteen contestants and photos of the top three contestants with all of the judges.

I still felt wobbly as I took my solo pictures with Cynthea Bey. This was way more attention and fanfare than I was used to. She was sweet about helping me to loosen up by making small talk and asking me what I planned to do with the prize money.

"I plan on registering for volleyball summer camp," I told her, loving the sound of that statement.

When the session was over, Cynthea thanked me for my patience.

"I'll see you on the dance floor." She flashed me her famous smile. "But for now, I think someone is waiting to spend time with you."

She looked behind me and I turned around to see Brent waiting in the wings.

"Why don't you come on over here and get in a shot with London?" You couldn't deny Didier when he boomed out a request that loud.

"Yeah." Asha laughed and immediately pulled the both of us onto the set, positioning us in front of the camera stand. "That's a great idea."

Brent and I were so embarrassed, but that didn't stop him from putting his arm around me in a warm, affectionate pose.

Gravity was pulling the volleyball down faster than I had anticipated. I timed my jump to meet the ball right over the net. With a quick open-handed swing, I fired the ball over the net with a burning slap. Through the net, I watched the ball blast the floorboards.

"That was a perfect shot!" Brent sounded too excited, considering no one was on the other side of the net. I was on the court solo. Still, I was flattered by his compliment.

"Thanks," I said.

"I wasn't talking about you, L." Brent didn't look up from the screen on his fancy camera. "I'm talking about yours truly. I timed that picture perfectly. Check this out."

He walked over with the screen angled so that I could get a better look at the action pic. The image of me looked like it was ready for a Nike billboard.

"Let's get another one," he instructed, running back to the sidelines and pointing his lens my way.

"Nah-uh," I protested. "That was my fourth one in a row."

"You trying to tell me you're tired?" he teased. "Miss Peak Performance?"

Brent was proud of me, and he couldn't stop bringing up my distinction any chance he got. Summer camp had handed out the accolades for its honorable mentions and I got a nod for rocking it out and challenging myself in my sports group.

I wasn't the only one busy working on a dream goal these days. Pam got permission from Cynthea Bey to post pictures from the opening night on her blog. Her site traffic peaked again. She hadn't turned the success of the blog into a successful T-shirt business yet, but other, more journalistic, doors were opening for her. Besides, Pam believed that the fact that her T-shirts weren't all over the place made it that much more exclusive and cool to own one.

I was happy for her. And I was so glad she and Jake had been spending a lot of time with Brent and me. There has never been a more ideal double-date situation in history.

Even though summer camp was an amazing experience, I was eager to get back to playing at school. The heart of the game beats more passionately there, in my opinion. Plus I was starting to appreciate the bond my teammates and I had. Junior year was going to be great because we were going to try to beat our record and make state championships. I thought we had a good chance.

Brent turned his back and then swiveled around in a quick James Bond move to snap an unexpected picture of me.

"Oh, I see how you wanna do this." I balanced the ball between my hip and my hand.

"I'm glad you do."

"But I'm a firm believer of *being* about it and not just talking about it," I continued.

"Nice to hear."

"So, why don't you come and see what it's like to jump up that high in the air four times in a row."

"That ain't nothin'." He was showboating as he placed his camera on the freshly shellacked floor and walked over, leaning back. "You're talking to someone who can dunk a basketball on a bad day, when my temperature is over a hundred and I just got off bed rest."

"Okay, rude *bwoy*," I said to fan the flames. "Let's see whatchu got."

Brent walked over and stood at the opposite side of the net. We stared at each other through the linked ropes. I tried not to laugh as I held my challenging stare. I couldn't look at him like I look at my opponents. He was too cute.

"Ready?" I asked him in the most serious tone I could muster. "I'm gonna spike and you try to block."

"Ain't no *thang* but a chicken *wang*," Brent said, acting like his favorite character from *Chappelle's Show*.

I shook my head.

"It's too bad you're about to get your hands burnt like you just gave the sun a soul-brotha handshake, because this ball is gonna be hot *fi-yah*."

"Stop talkin' 'bout it and be 'bout it," he said with widened eyes.

With that, I threw the ball high in the air, and as it made its way back to me, I jumped up with my arm raised and whipped my palm out to meet it about a foot above the net.

Brent didn't time his jump as well as I did. But he was right; he jumped as if he had springs in his sneakers. Unfortunately, he wasn't as graceful in staying upright.

In his hunger to prove how high he could jump, Brent overextended. As soon as he was off the ground, his body angled toward the net. The closeness of the net spooked him, so in an attempt to avoid hitting it, Brent lost his footing and clumsily fell to the ground.

"Oooh! Are you all right?" I asked. "Because you know I can't crack up at how hilarious that looked until I know you're okay."

He rolled from his side to his back, holding a hand out to me. I tugged but he tugged harder. I tumbled on top of him in a fit of laughter. He rolled me over to his side, laughing.

I dragged out my giggles for longer than he did. Brent sobered up and pulled me closer to him. My laughter faded to a chuckle and then to a smile.

That's when Brent cupped the side of my face with his hand, lowering his head to mine, and kissed me.

Right there under the net.

About the Author

Debbie Rigaud began her writing career covering news and entertainment for magazines. She's interviewed celebs, politicians, and social figures, but enjoyed interviewing "real" girls the best. Her writing has appeared in *Seventeen*, *CosmoGIRL!*, *Twist*, *J-14*, *Essence*, *Trace*, and *Heart & Soul*. Debbie's novella *Double Act* is featured in the YA anthology *Hallway Diaries*. A total Jersey girl, Debbie now lives in Bermuda with her husband. For more information, visit www.debbierigaud.com.

"I would've asked for this in a sippy cup if I'd known you were going to be driving the Saab," Becca said the next morning as we headed for the Sunporch Café. She attempted another sip of her caramel latte just as I wrestled the car into second. A wave of amber liquid baptized her Seven skinny jeans. "Damn, Val!" she exclaimed.

"Hey, at least we even have a car to drive today," I said, fighting with the clutch. "Mom was threatening to take it grocery shopping, but I talked her out of it." At the next red light I remembered to press the clutch before stomping the brake and gingerly easing the Saab into neutral.

"Yeah, I feel *so* lucky the Beemer's in the shop," Becca muttered. She had a blob of whipped cream on her upper lip. It made her look like a transvestite Charlie Chaplin.

The light turned green and I took a deep breath. Foot on clutch and brake, then off brake and on the clutch, shift into first, press on accelerator, then foot off clutch but carefully. A fire truck began wailing just behind me and roared past as I slammed my foot on the brake, forgetting the clutch, of course. "Shit!" The Saab jolted across the intersection in big bronco bucks.

"Hel-help, hel-help," Becca jerked out, holding on to her coffee with both hands.

"Hang on, I've got it now," I said just as the motor stalled.

"Val, get us the hell out of here!" Becca yelled, staring at the line of cars forming on either side of us. I could hear a few ominous honks.

"I'm trying!" I forced myself to breathe before I shifted into neutral again and carefully eased into first. Bing. The Saab crept smoothly across the intersection as if it had never stalled in its life.

"So," Becca breathed. "Are you going to tell me about that madness online last night?"

I grinned. "No, wait until we get there. Then I can explain it to both of you at once." I braked hard as the green awning of the Sunporch suddenly loomed in front of me. The car slewed sideways and wound up in a parking space, bumper first. "Hey, look, right in front!" I chortled as I climbed from the car.

"You're three feet from the curb!" Becca protested. She stared at the wide gap of asphalt in dismay.

"Whatever! Let's go, I'm starving." I could see Kelly through the window waving to us from a table. "I need some eggs Benedict, like, right now."

The steamy fragrance of frying bacon hit me full in the face as we pulled open the glass doors. Sunlight flooded the little restaurant, pouring in the big front windows and spreading in pools on the gleaming wooden floor. All around was the pleasant murmur and clink of breakfast, punctuated by the ring of the cash register up front.

"Okay, talk, you," Kelly ordered the moment we slid into our seats. Her wet hair was pulled back in a loose braid, and her skin was fresh and rosy. Three orange juices stood at our places.

"Oh my God, please don't tell me you've already been running," Becca moaned as she opened the huge plastic-covered menu. "It's ten o'clock on Saturday!"

Kelly shrugged. "I only did five miles."

Becca rolled her eyes and looked up as a

waitress with a shaved head and big plastic plugs in her earlobes appeared by our table. "I'll have the banana chocolate-chip pancakes with whipped cream, a side of bacon, and two eggs, scrambled. Thanks."

"Just oatmeal for me and a grapefruit," Kelly said. "And coffee with skim milk."

Becca's glare practically burned a hole in the booth behind Kelly's head. "You know, I think I'll have a side of hashbrowns also," Becca said to the punked-out server.

Kelly smiled sweetly. "Actually, no milk with the coffee. Black is fine."

I sighed. Another morning with passive-aggressive food competition. "Eggs Benedict," I said. The waitress nodded, blank-faced, and scribbled on her pad before walking away.

"Okay!" Kelly turned to me like a woman on a mission. "Talk, crazy lady."

I grinned and took a leisurely sip of orange juice. The girls leaned forward across the table.

"Come on!" Becca said. "You're driving us crazy. What was the deal with all that weird stuff about Violet?"

"Viola," I corrected. "Remember, the girl in *Twelfth Night*?"

They both stared at me blankly.

"See, Viola gets shipwrecked and she's all alone, so—"

"Whatever!" Becca cut me off. "Are you out of your gourd?"

I leaned back in my chair. The sun streaming in the window was warm on my face. "I'm one hundred percent sane. It's just like I said. I'm swearing off guys until school lets out. It's perfect—for the first time since eighth grade, there'll be no boys in my life at all. I mean, not romantically. It's a brilliant plan."

"Until school ends," Kelly said.

"Right. I want to see how it feels to be totally on my own, instead of always either dealing with a boyfriend or looking for one."

"Is this all because of Dave?" Becca asked.

"Partly. But it's also everything that's been happening at school. All the attention from guys is really getting on my nerves. Maybe checking out for a while would give me a new perspective on things."

Kelly pursed her mouth up. "What about flirting?"

I shook my head. "No flirting."

"What about just *talking*?" Becca asked.

I thought. "I guess talking is okay. I mean, like, my chem lab partner is a guy and I have to talk to him. And telling Willy I can't go out with him for the gazillionth time, that would be okay."

"For a whole semester." Kelly narrowed her eyes.

"Right." The waitress set down our food and I took a bite of my eggs Benedict. The hollandaise was silky and delicious.

We were silent for a minute, and then Kelly burst out laughing.

"What?" I asked.

"This is impossible! You won't be able to do it. For one thing, no one can go a whole semester without at least *flirting*. For another thing, you've always had a boyfriend, Ms. Valerie M. Rushford, remember? Just like we were talking about at Becca's." She pointed her spoon at me like a fencing sword. Little blobs of oatmeal dripped off it.

"So? A person can change, can't she?" I said, poking at another piece of egg. It slid out from under my fork and flew off the plate, landing on the front of Becca's pink cashmere sweater.

"Val!" Becca dabbed at the egg. "Look,

sure a person can change. But why are you being so extreme? Why not just say, 'I'm not going to go out with anyone for a while?' Why all the rules?" She dipped her napkin in her water and scrubbed at her front.

"Sorry about that," I said.

"Well, don't be sorry. I mean, I'm just giving you my opinion—"

"No! I meant sorry about the egg." I leaned forward. "And as far as all the rules, I mean, I have to have a plan if I'm going to do this. If there aren't any rules, I might screw it up. And you guys know—if I'm going to do something, then I'm going to do it right. No half-assing." I waved my fork at them. "I thought you guys were my supportive friends, huh? Whatever happened to that?"

"We *are* supportive," Becca soothed. "It's just that this seems kind of . . ."

"Crazy?" Kelly suggested.

I heaved a disgusted sigh. "Look, just trust me. It's going to be great."

"Yeah, but this is totally out of character for you," Kelly insisted. "You wouldn't even know how to do it."

"Nuns do it all the time." Becca ran the last piece of pancake around on her plate.

"But Val's not a nun," Kelly pointed out. They both looked at me.

"Maybe you should think about becoming a nun," Becca said.

"Guys! I'm not becoming a nun. I'm just swearing off dating. Like detoxing. I'm going to get it out of my system so I don't make another mistake like Dave." I looked from one skeptical face to the other. Then I slid my plate to one side and flipped over my paper place mat, dotted here and there with hollandaise. I extracted a pen from my bag. "All right. I can see you guys aren't convinced I'm serious." At the top of the place mat I wrote, *Val's Grand Dating Plan*.

"What are you doing?" Becca asked. She craned her neck across the table.

"I'm making it official." *Number 1,* I wrote. *No dates—not with guys, girls, frogs, or princes.* I slid the paper around so the others could see.

Kelly read it and nodded. "So far, so good."

Number 2, I continued. *No flirting—arm touches, cute smiles, hair tossing, etc. Number 3, No romance—no gifts, love notes, kissing, holding hands. This plan is binding until the last day of school. I hereby swear to it.* I signed my name with a flourish and shoved it across the table.

Kelly grabbed it. "Wow, a contract! All right, Val, you're on." She folded the place mat and stuck it inside a library book in her bag.

"So, when are you going to begin the GDP?" Becca swiped her finger through the syrup pooling on her plate.

"GDP?" I asked.

"'Grand Dating Plan.'"

"How about tonight?" Kelly suggested, a little smile curling the edges of her lips.

"But your house party is tonight," Becca pointed out. Kelly always threw the first party after we got back from spring break, and it was always awesome. Everyone from school would be there.

"So?" Kelly's voice was tough. She stared at me with one eyebrow slightly raised.

I stared back and lifted my chin. "Tonight's fine. Great, in fact. I was just thinking I should get started right away."

Stupid Cupid

*Make a date
with Felicity*

and look for:

**Flirting
with
Disaster**

From Simon Pulse ♥ Published by Simon & Schuster

Want to hear what the Romantic Comedies authors are doing when they are not writing books?

Check out
PulseRoCom.com
to see the authors blogging together, plus get sneak peeks of upcoming titles!

check your PULSE

Simon & Schuster's **Check Your Pulse**
e-newsletter delivers current updates on
the hottest titles, exciting sweepstakes, and
exclusive content from your favorite authors.

Visit **TEEN.SimonandSchuster.com** to
sign up, post your thoughts, and find out what
every avid reader is talking about!

Margaret K. McElderry Books

Simon & Schuster
Books for Young Readers

SIMON PULSE